Orlando

Channing

Tyrone

Beyonsay

THOSE KIDS NEXT DOOR! 2

Sylvester

Arthur

Ma

Margaret

Copyright © Alan Stott 2019
Illustrations © Terry Cooper 2019

Published by
Candy Jar Books
Mackintosh House
136 Newport Road, Cardiff, CF24 1DJ
www.candyjarbooks.co.uk

ISBN: 978-1-912535-54-5

Edited by Shaun Russell & Keren Williams

Printed and bound in the UK by
Severn, Bristol Road, Gloucester, GL2 5EU

Best wishes

Alan Scott

This book is dedicated to my four grandchildren,
Barney, Franklin, Hatti and Albie, who continue
to present me with Shufflett situations!

And to Shaun Russell whose counselling and
inspiration continually help me to develop as a writer.
Terry Cooper for making the characters look real.

My very supportive family and, in
particular, my wife, Jacqueline.

RESIDENTS SCRAMBLE AS EGGS THROWN!

More than a dozen people were pelted with eggs yesterday as residents gathered to watch City Council members evict a troublesome family from a local housing estate.

The family, who cannot be named for legal reasons, has been moved several times previously due to causing trouble with neighbours. Wherever they are placed, complaints come pouring in to the Council offices.

The mother of the five children refused to comment and the father has not been seen for almost two years.

Next door neighbour, Mrs Ava Grumpold, 68, told our reporter, "They are wild!" Another neighbour, Mrs Florence Mildew, 63, said, "They are out of control if you ask me."

Recently, the children have run a reign of terror setting fire to a shed, pouring blue paint over cars and the pavement, and stealing food from a resident's shopping bag.

In a final attempt to get rid of the problems, The Council has bought a property many miles away in the Welsh countryside where the family has now been sent to live.

"We are sending them where they cannot do any more harm to anyone." Mr Snodgrass, 48, Leader of the Council stated. 'Their only neighbours now will be cows and sheep!"

True to their bad reputation, the family managed one more act of defiance during the eviction. As the removal van set off, a barrage of eggs were thrown by the children at anyone standing close enough to be a target. Mr Snodgrass and Mrs Frazzle, 43, were the first to be egged.

Wiping egg from his neck and shirt as the van drew away, Mr Bernard Wegley, 84, said, "I would have preferred a cream egg! But this is a great day for us to see the back of that lot. They burned my shed down!"

The residents now hope to settle back to their peaceful neighbourhood and the Council members are confident that they will never have to deal with the family again.

REPORTER: VERITY RUSSELL

CHAPTER ONE
Bear With
a Sore Head

Beyonsay waddled to the stairgate at the top of the stairs in a way that only young babies can waddle. She lifted a football high above her head, and stood up on her toes to push that little bit higher.

'Bor,' she said. 'Tairs.'

The ball sat on top of the gate, held in place by Beyonsay's tiny fingertips. 'Bor,' she repeated. 'Tairs.'

The ball remained still.

Then Beyonsay made one last flick with her fingers and it rolled slowly over the top.

She giggled with delight.

'Bor. Tairs.'

She watched the ball drop onto the first stair and bounce back up.

She clapped her hands as the ball began to fall again. This time it landed about half way down before bouncing back up. Then, for a third time it was on its way down and, **THIS** time, it would **NOT** bounce back up.

Beyonsay pushed her face between the bars of the stairgate, watching the movement of the ball in wonder. 'Bor! Tairs,' she said with a giggle.

Across the hall, just by the door, there stood a tall wooden vase stand.

With a vase on it.

A glass vase.

With hundreds of tiny coloured pebbles inside.

Doing nothing.

The ball landed perfectly on the edge of the bottom stair, shot across the hall in a straight line, and bounced off the vase stand. Two of its four legs lifted off the floor.

The stand teetered one way, then the other. It hovered **drunkenly** on two legs, before rocking back the other way.

Then, in slow motion, the vase began to **PLUMMET** towards the wooden floor. Beyonsay did not know it, but this was going to be spectacular. The vase hit the floor with an astonishingly loud

CRASH!

It burst open and a thousand pebbles scattered all over the floor, bouncing and dancing, sounding like

sparklers on Bonfire Night.

Beyonsay gripped the gate tight with both hands, jumping up and down excitedly. She did not seem to care about the carnage at the bottom of the stairs. 'Bor gone,' she said. 'Bor gone.'

Sylvester was the first to appear. He looked down the stairs, **HORRIFIED** at the devastation. Beyonsay looked up at him with both palms facing upwards. 'Bor gone,' she said. 'Bor gone.'

Ma arrived seconds later, scooping Beyonsay up in both arms and hugging her tightly. She was not concerned with anything else. Channing came running out of her room convinced that half the house had collapsed. Tyrone stood silently in his doorway, holding Teddy tightly to his face. Orlando was nowhere to be seen!

'Everybody stay up here! Do *not* go downstairs. I need to go down and clean up this mess,' hollered Ma. The children did as they were told and stood watching behind the gate as Ma dutifully cleaned up. It took nearly twenty minutes until Ma declared the hall safe to walk through. 'Better wear your slippers,' she said.

'Just in case.'

Channing was the first to brave it. She wondered where Orlando could be, and why he had not appeared during all this commotion.

She skipped lightly down the stairs and across the hall to the kitchen, humming to herself. She was happy. Today was going to be such fun. Orlando and Sylvester were going to visit Arthur and Margaret next door. They were going to apologise. This she **had** to see!

Orlando sat at the table looking extremely glum, his elbows resting on the table and his head sandwiched between his hands. His breakfast remained untouched. He had been sitting there for some time, deep in concentration. Downcast.

'Have you been here all the time?' Channing asked.

Orlando completely ignored her.

'Can you hear me?' she said, prodding him.

Nothing.

'Are you sulking?'

No response.

'You look like a bear with a sore head!' Channing

said with a smirk.

'Mind your own business!' he hurled back.

'Ooh, touchy too!' she persisted.

'How do you know what a bear with a sore head looks like anyway?'

'Easy. It looks like **YOU!**'

Orlando launched himself at his sister, and they fell, sprawling, onto the kitchen floor. Just then Ma arrived carrying Beyonsay who giggled at them.

Ma's reaction was very different. 'Get up or you'll both get a clip!' she said loudly with a grunt.

'*He* started it!' yelled Channing, getting to her feet.

'*You* did. You called me a bear...'

Ma cut him short. 'One more sound from either of you and you'll spend the rest of the day in your bedrooms.'

The twins scowled at each other – something they were very good at.

Ma strapped Beyonsay into her high chair and gave her a bottle of juice. 'Now drink up your juice,' she said.

'Hooss!' Beyonsay gurgled.

'Juice,' Ma prompted, smiling.

'Hooss!' Beyonsay repeated and giggled. 'Hooss!'

The twins laughed through their scowls. 'Hooss,' they both said, together and everyone laughed.

'Right!' said Ma. The twins knew that an announcement was imminent. 'I think you have some unfinished business, Orlando.'

Orlando knew exactly what she meant. 'What do you mean, Ma?' he asked with the best, most innocent, angelic expression he could muster.

'You know very well what I mean. You're going to apologise to Arthur and Margaret. Remember?'

'What? But...'

'Go and get Sylvester and we will all go together. I want to make sure that you apologise properly.'

'You don't need to come with us, Ma. We can do it on our own.'

'Not a chance!' said Ma. 'I'm coming with you to make sure you do it.'

Channing mocked Orlando from behind Ma's back, silently giggling.

'Pff!' Orlando felt all of his energy drain away and

he resembled a bear with a sore head – **again.**
Getting caught was the risk you took when you did
something daring. Orlando was daring. He *never* did
anything wrong (or naughty) – only daring. And he
hated being caught. **There was no fun in that!**

But this was different. He was being forced to go
and apologise to Arthur when *Arthur* should be the
one apologising to *HIM*! Arthur had pelted them with
blue pellets that really hurt. *And* made a mess of their
clothes!

Orlando did not like apologising, but that wasn't
the reason he felt so bad about meeting Arthur again.
The real reason was that Arthur was *better* than him
with a catapult! In fact, Orlando had never seen
anyone so fast and accurate. And Arthur was an *old*
man. Little did he realise that this *'old man'* would
continue to surprise him more and more over the next
few days.

'Right. Move,' Ma ordered.

Orlando trudged upstairs. 'Sylvie! Let's go. She
hasn't forgotten.'

Sylvester launched himself at Orlando's chest.

'Don't call me Sylvie!' he yelled, and they crashed into the wall, before falling to the floor, wrestling and aiming punches at each other.

'Don't make me come and get you!' Ma shouted.

Ten minutes later the family knocked on the door of Oak Cottage. Beyonsay sat gurgling in her pushchair and Ma, holding Tyrone's hand, gazed through the kitchen window. Ma looked determined. Channing watched as the boys shared awkward glances with each other. They looked grim. Channing smiled, revelling in their discomfort.

In the house Margaret sat knitting and Arthur was reading a book. Arthur peered over his reading glasses.

'Don't rush. Let them wait a little. It will make them feel worse,' he said with a sly grin. Margaret could tell that Arthur was going to love this.

'Oh, you are cruel!' Margaret chided.

'It will certainly make them think twice before

upsetting anyone again,' Arthur said, more in hope than certainty.

Margaret stole a quick glance through the kitchen door window. 'It looks like they've *all* come round. The whole family. We'd better put the kettle on.'

'What? All of them?' He followed her gaze.

Margaret opened the door. 'Hello, everyone,' she said, sporting a weak smile. 'It's lovely to see you. And so many of you, too! Please do come in.' She stood back as the horde stumbled into the kitchen, with Ma pulling Beyonsay's pushchair up the step backwards.

Ma took the opportunity to **SCOWL** at Orlando and Sylvester. They knew the look. She turned to Margaret and smiled. 'Oh Margaret, your kitchen is beautiful,' she said. 'What do *you* think, Channing?'

'I love it,' she answered, looking around. 'It's massive.' Margaret looked quite pleased with the compliment.

'What do *you* think, boys?' Ma smiled at the two villains, drawing them into the conversation completely against their will.

'Erm, lovely,' muttered Sylvester.

'Pff,' was all Orlando could muster.

Arthur looked at Ma, studying her carefully. Was she deliberately making her boys squirm? He held back a smile. **IT WAS OBVIOUS THAT MA MEANT BUSINESS.**

'Please, do take a seat,' Margaret said, as she walked them through into a very spacious lounge. They all sat down, and Arthur said, 'Would you like a cup of tea, Mrs...?'

'Shufflett,' said Ma with a nod. 'But please, call me Becky.'

'Becky it is,' he answered. 'One tea for you and would the children like squash?'

'Yes pl—'

'No, they can all have water,' Ma interrupted. 'It's better for their teeth.'

'Water it is,' Arthur added. He was beginning to like Ma. **SHE WAS DECISIVE.**

Arthur brought the drinks on a tray and everyone sat in silence for a moment.

Then Ma broke the tension, 'So, boys, you've got something special to say to Arthur and Margaret, haven't you?' She **glared** at them, compelling them not to try anything clever.

Once again all Orlando could say was, 'Pff!'

'**No-o-o**,' said Ma with a smile. She exaggerated the word as she said it. 'I thought we were going to speak to them in English, remember? We practised English before we got here.'

'Sorry,' said Sylvester. Ma gave him a glare of encouragement to carry on. 'I'm *very* sorry for what we did yesterday.' She looked satisfied and gave him a nod.

Everyone stared at Orlando. He could feel their eyes burning into him. He knew that if he waited any longer, he would not be able to do this, so he blurted out very loudly **'SO-RRY!'** and continued looking at his feet.

Arthur and Margaret exchanged glances. Apologising had obviously been very difficult for Orlando.

'I know how they can both repay us,' Arthur said

with a hint of a smile. He winked at Ma and she smiled back at him.

Orlando looked at him in horror. *What?* He had just apologised. *Wasn't that enough?! What more did he want?* 'I've just said 'sorry'!' He was apoplectic!

'I've not had a chance to clean the hens because of the rain. It would be a real act of kindness if you two lads mucked out the hen coop. Follow me and I'll show you what to do.'

Orlando, eyes wide open, looked in dismay for an excuse. 'But... but, I don't know. I've never done that before... I can't... I've got my best clothes on... urgh!'

'Oh, don't worry about that,' said Arthur. 'Chicken poo is nowhere near as bad as cow poo! That's *MUCH* smellier! And stickier!'

Ma held her hand to her mouth to cover her laughter. She looked at Margaret who was also laughing silently.

Five minutes later Arthur came back in chuckling. 'That should put a stop to their mischief.' He grinned. 'I've shown them what to do and left them to it.'

He turned to Channing and Tyrone. 'Who are

these fine-looking children?'

'This is Channing,' Ma said. 'She and Orlando are twins. I'm sorry but I don't know your surname, Arthur. What would you prefer the children to call you?'

'It's Revell, Arthur and Margaret Revell,' Arthur pointed out, 'but please let them call us Arthur and Margaret. Everyone else does.'

'OK. Say "hello" to Arthur, Channing.'

'Hello, Arthur,' Channing said. 'Hello, Margaret.'

Ma looked at Tyrone. 'Hello, Arthur,' Tyrone said, squeezing his teddy and hiding his face in Ma's lap. He went bright red.

'Hello, Fartur,' said Beyonsay. 'Hello, Fartur.'

Everyone fell about laughing.

And from that moment onwards – for the first time in his life – Arthur became known as Artur the farter.

CHAPTER TWO
Scooping Poo

Hen poo comes in many different colours, but this poo was mostly brown and white. Some poo is dry and **lumpy,** but much of this poo was wet and **sticky!**

The smell was more than the boys could stomach. Sylvester was holding his nose and Orlando had his camouflage jacket up over his face. Both boys were trying to hold their breath.

They stared in disbelief at the **smelly**, *soggy*, **WET** straw inside the chicken coop. 'This stinks!' said Orlando. 'I'm *never* going to eat another egg in my life – *ever.*'

They began raking the straw into a pile. The more

they raked, the smellier it became. Some broken eggs added to the sticky mess and their misery. Orlando grabbed a shovel and began scooping the pile into a black bin liner held open by Sylvester.

He was not very accurate. The cold straw mess dragged across Sylvester's hands.

'Aaargh!' screamed Sylvester. He dropped the bag, spilling everything over his shoes and trousers. He looked down with revulsion and a look of disgust on his face.

His shoes were covered in poo.

His trousers were covered in poo.

His hands were covered in poo.

His coat was clean!

For the first time that day, Orlando burst out laughing!

What the heck, Sylvester thought. And he wiped his hands on his coat! Orlando laughed louder!

Sylvester stared at him, wondering what to do.

Angrily he picked up a pile of messy straw and hurled it at Orlando. It splattered on Orlando's camouflage jacket!

In retaliation, Orlando scooped up a huge bundle of soggy, **smelly** straw and threw it at Sylvester's head. Sylvester ducked, slipped, fell backwards and landed in the disgusting mess on the ground.

'**Nooooo!**' Sylvester shouted. He spotted two eggs next to him, grabbed them gratefully and launched them both at Orlando.

The first one landed on Orlando's chest and exploded with a POOFFF! The second one caught him full on the forehead. **SPLAT!**

The next few minutes were a whirlwind as both brothers hurled straw at each other – laughing as they did so. And, for the second time in only a few days, they looked like scarecrows!

'Enough!' called Orlando, at last. 'We had better get cleaned up and finish this job.'

Together they swept the straw from the shelves. Some hens would not move and cackled angrily when they tried to **shoo** them away.

'They could be laying eggs,' Orlando observed.

'Which are the hens we put inside Raj's van?' asked Sylvester, looking around.

'I don't know. They all look the same to me,' Orlando answered.

'Hey. Wait a minute, look at these.' He pointed to several eggs nestling in the straw.

'Oh, now that's lucky,' Orlando deliberated.

'Yeah, it's lucky we didn't push them into the bag with the rubbish. They would have been—' Sylvester stopped when he noticed a strange smirk on Orlando's face.

'No, I don't mean that. I mean that it's lucky for *us* that we found them. Do you understand?'

Sylvester read the look in his brother's eyes. 'Now I know what you mean.' He grinned as he realised what Orlando had in mind.

'Let's find some more,' Orlando encouraged, and the two boys set about searching carefully and thoroughly for more eggs.

After a further two minutes, they had collected seven eggs and had hidden them under a bush. They quickly placed clean straw on the shelves and floor, and closed the coop after them.

Ten minutes later everybody was heading back to Budleigh Cottage. 'Now that's the end of it. Do you understand, you two?' Ma said with a hiss.

'Yes, Ma,' they both replied with a grin that Ma did not see.

'I don't want any more trouble with those two lovely people. Is that clear?'

'Yes, Ma. Clear as daylight,' Orlando replied, smirking. Channing spotted the smirk and knew that Orlando had something in his mind but, at this moment, could not tell what it was.

When they arrived back at Budleigh, the boys were ordered upstairs to shower and change their clothes.

'Yeah. Get those clothes off, you *stink!*' Channing added with delight.

'You **stink!**' Tyrone joined in.

'*Tink!*' added Beyonsay and they all laughed.

Fifteen minutes later, smelling clean and looking tidy,

the two boys arrived in the kitchen where Ma had prepared some lunch. While they were eating they heard strange noises coming from outside.

'That sounds like cows,' Channing said, starting to get up to go and look.

'Nobody move!' growled Ma. 'Until you've finished.'

'What do cows do, Bee?' Channing asked, looking at Beyonsay who was sitting in her high chair with yoghurt all over her face and bib.

'MOO,' said Beyonsay, and they all laughed.

'MOO!' Tyrone joined in, and everyone laughed again.

'Her name is Beyonsay, not Bee,' Ma reminded them, adding, 'don't you dare *moo*-ve until you have finished eating and tidied up.' She smiled at her little joke and the children laughed with her.

'Nobody **moooo-ve**!' Tyrone dragged the word out long and loud, then everybody joined in, 'Nobody **moooo-ve**!'

The mooing outside continued until they had finished their lunch. It was torture to the Shufflett children who were desperate to see what was happening outside.

'OK,' said Ma, putting away the last of the dishes. 'Go and have a look.'

Channing picked up Beyonsay and followed the boys outside. The mooing was coming from a barn just about eighty metres away from the cottage. They hadn't really taken much notice of it until now. So, quickly they headed over to see a huge herd of very young cows staring at them from behind a metal gate. They were mostly **black** and white and their eyes were large and very black. The cows pushed forward, staring intently at the children.

'What are they?' Tyrone asked. 'Are they cows?'

'Elephants,' Channing replied jokingly. She did not think that he would believe her.

'Yes, elephants without trunks,' Orlando said, joining in.

'Where are their trunks?'

'They've sent them to the cleaners,' Channing replied.

Sylvester whispered, 'They are cows, Tyrone.'

'Cows? I thought so, but they are so big!' Tyrone responded. 'Look, Teddy. Cows.'

Just then, one of the cows lifted its tail high and produced an ENORMOUS dark brown, squelching poo.

Splat!

It landed with a whooshing sound and looked like a **MASSIVE** pancake.

'Well excuse me, please!' Orlando said, pretending to be shocked.

'Don't they have any toilets around here?' Sylvester said, as he joined in disapprovingly.

'Look, Bee, aren't they pretty?' Beyonsay squealed

with delight.

The children were surprised to see that the calves were as tall as the twins. As they got closer to the gate, the young cows SNORTED and backed away shyly, without blinking and without taking their eyes off them. It was as if they knew what these kids next door were like.

The air smelled very strange but sweet, and it was cold enough to see the breath coming from some of the cows like steam from a kettle.

Orlando and Sylvester leaned on the gate and Channing lifted Beyonsay onto her shoulders for a better view. Beyonsay was enchanted. 'Moo!' she imitated, 'MOO!'

The calves snorted and sniffed back at her. Their HUGE eyes were still fixed on the children. Orlando picked some grass and held it in his outstretched hand towards the calves. 'Come here,' he said. 'Come and get some lovely fresh grass.'

Two cows began to inch towards him, but were much too shy to take the grass.

Beyonsay giggled and leaned forward to put both

hands under Channing's chin. She squeezed too tightly, almost choking Channing who began laughing and coughing. 'Don't choke me, Bee!' she said with a wheeze.

Beyonsay bounced up and down on Channing's shoulders, 'MOO! MOO! MOO!'

'Bee, calm down!' Channing blurted. Beyonsay now had her hands over Channing's eyes and she could not see anything.

The calves seemed captivated by the children. Slowly a few of the more confident ones moved forward towards the gate, intrigued.

'Are they boys or girls?' Sylvester asked.

'They're boys,' replied Channing, pulling Beyonsay's hands away from her eyes.

'Yeah, they're boys,' agreed Orlando.

'How do you know?' Sylvester continued, curious by this.

'They've got none of them pink things at the back. You know – like Ma's pink washing up gloves,' Orlando added perceptively.

'Do cows wear washing up gloves?' Tyrone said,

joining in the conversation.

'Only when they wash the dishes.' Orlando was beginning to have some fun.

'No, Tyrone.' Channing said kindly, glaring hard at Orlando. 'They have them things at the back that look like upside down pink rubber gloves. It's called an udder.'

'And only the girls have them,' Orlando added. 'That's an-udder fact for you to remember!' He laughed loudly.

'And an-udder fact is that boy cows are called bullocks.' Orlando was really enjoying himself now.

Sylvester had climbed up on the gate and was sitting on the top bar with his feet over the other side of the gate. As the cows at the back pushed forward, the front ones were forced nearer. Sylvester held the bar with one hand and reached out to stroke the nearest bullock.

Unfortunately the bar was **wet** and **slimy** and his hand slipped off. In order to save himself from falling into the cow poo, Sylvester launched himself into the air and landed on the back of the nearest cow which immediately freaked out.

MOO-UUUUUUGH!

The cow turned and began to push its way through the others. Sylvester clung on to its neck. **'AAAAAAAGH!** Help me!' he shouted. At the far end of the barn there was an open door leading out onto the field where the cows grazed. The cow headed for the field, bellowing all the way. Sylvester hung on with his arms around its neck, screaming all the way.

Beyonsay giggled and clapped her hands enthusiastically.

Channing looked on, horrified.

Tyrone hid behind his teddy, too frightened to look.

Orlando ran to the side of the barn and giggled as the cow emerged and raced up the field with Sylvester clinging on for life. The cow was still bellowing and Sylvester was still screaming.

'Ma! Orlando! Help me!'

Suddenly the cow stopped and Sylvester was catapulted over its head.

Now cows don't have toilets. They poo anywhere in the field. Lots of cows do lots of poos and this field was full of **POO.** Big, wet pancakes of dirty brown poo.

And Sylvester was on his way down. Into a massive cow pat!

Squelch!

He slid for half a metre.

In the poo! On his back! The cold, slimy poo was forced up into his coat and jumper and all over his back.

Orlando ran up to him laughing but Sylvester was not in the mood.

'I hate this place!' he yelled. 'There's poo everywhere! Why have we got to live here?'

Walking back to the house was the worst thing Sylvester had ever done. The poo had started to dry and he could only walk like a robot. Orlando was trying to help, but he did not want to get poo on himself, so he didn't try too hard.

While Sylvester was in the bath getting cleaned up, Orlando grabbed his football and went in search of some action. He walked up the lane dribbling the ball. Then he kicked it a few metres in front of him and waited for it to roll back down the hill to him.

Before long, he found himself outside Arthur's

drive. He walked down the drive, calmly bouncing his football until he stood outside Arthur's workshop. A motor sound was coming from inside. He decided to see what was happening and peered in through the door.

Arthur was bent over a LARGE machine. There was a piece of wood spinning and Arthur seemed to be changing its shape. The machine was making an incredibly **LOUD** noise and he was wearing ear protectors.

'What are you doing, Arthur?' Orlando called.

Nothing.

'What are you doing, Arthur?'

Still nothing.

Orlando realised that Arthur could not hear him, so he walked up to him and touched his arm.

Arthur leapt into the air! His eyes wide open in surprise behind a pair of protective goggles. He reached for the button to turn off the machine.

'Oh, you gave me a fright,' he said, as the noise of the motor slowly died away.

'What are you doing, Arthur?'

'I'm making a wooden fruit bowl for one of my friends,' he answered. Arthur explained that the machine was a lathe, and he was making the bowl using a chisel. Orlando was not very interested in bowls and looked around. He spotted a rectangular wooden shape on the work bench.

'What's this?' he asked.

'That's a photo frame I'm making for someone else,' replied Orlando.

'How do the pieces stick together?'

'I use super glue,' Arthur informed him.

'What's super glue?'

'It's a very strong, quick-acting glue. It sticks two things together in under ten seconds!'

'*Wow*! That's fast!' said Orlando, intrigued.

'You have to be very careful or it will stick your fingers together!' Arthur smiled. 'And you don't want that to happen, do you?'

'Has it ever happened to you, Arthur?'

'No, not yet, I'm glad to say,' Arthur responded. 'But several people have had to go to hospital to get their fingers unstuck!'

'Wow!' Orlando said thoughtfully. 'It's powerful then.'

Orlando had the ball under his arm.

'Can you do anything with that ball?' asked Arthur.

Orlando seemed a little startled by the question.

'Oh... er... Yes, I can do, erm, a hundred keepy uppies,' he lied magnificently.

'A hundred?' Arthur said, impressed. 'Can you show me?'

Orlando froze. 'Er, no, er, I... haven't got my boots on.'

'You don't need boots to do keepy uppies do you?' Arthur persisted. He could see that Orlando was feeling a little awkward.

'Oh yes, it's very important to have the right gear on,' Orlando added.

ARTHUR SMILED A LITTLE. Not enough for Orlando to see though. He knew that Orlando could not do a hundred keepy uppies, or he would have been very keen to show him. But he did not want to embarrass the boy, so he said, 'OK, will you show me next time when you've got your boots on?'

'Oh yes, no problem,' said Orlando, very relieved. Quickly changing the subject, Orlando picked up a small tool and asked, 'What's this for?'

'That's a chisel for shaping wood,' Arthur answered.

'And what is this?'

'That's a five-metre tape measure.'

'What about this?'

'That's a clamp for holding things together while I glue them.'

Orlando laughed when Floss bounded into the shed, woofing and trying to lick him. Orlando bent down to try to cuddle the dog, except that she did not want to be cuddled. She wanted to leap up and down very excitedly. Orlando curled into a ball and let her run around him, woofing and nibbling at his clothes and ears. *This is fun*, he thought.

A minute or two later, when she had calmed down a bit, Arthur said, 'Orlando, watch this. Floss, fetch me the glue gun.' She immediately turned and came back carrying Arthur's glue gun. She gave it to him gently. 'Good girl,' he said. 'Now, fetch me the paint brush.'

She returned with a paintbrush in her mouth and delicately handed it to Arthur. 'You are a good girl. Now fetch me the string.' She came back with a small ball of string. **ORLANDO WAS ENCHANTED.**

'This is the best one. Watch this. Floss, fetch me the broom.' Arthur looked at Orlando and winked to signal that this was going to be funny.

Floss took the broom handle sideways in her mouth. She could not lift it completely and began to drag it across the floor. It was too wide and too heavy for her and she began **knocking** things over in her determination to take it to Arthur. They both laughed as she knocked over two piles of wood and had to duck as they toppled towards her.

Five minutes later, Orlando was saying goodbye to Arthur, and was about to set off back home when he spotted a large brown plastic bottle next to a bin in the corner. It said wood glue on the side.

'Gosh, you have got a lot of glue, haven't you?'

'Yes, but that bottle is empty. I threw it at the bin and missed,' Arthur laughed.

Orlando suddenly became interested. 'Oh, don't

you need it any more?'

'No, I've got a new bottle.'

'Could I have it, Arthur?'

'Yes, of course. What are you going to do with it?'

'Maybe make a rocket with it.' But Orlando had other, special, plans for this bottle of glue. *And* the small container that he had **sneekily** taken off Arthur's bench and hidden in his pocket. He picked it up. 'Bye,' he said, and he was gone.

Arthur turned and spotted Orlando's ball on the floor. 'Orlando,' he shouted, 'you've forgotten your ball!'

Arthur dragged the ball back with his foot and with a deft touch, flicked it up onto his head and did five headers, before allowing it to drop onto his left foot and doing several juggles from foot to foot, before **FLICKING** it up into his hand. Orlando appeared at the door and Arthur threw the ball to him.

'Oh, thanks,' he said.

'It was my pleasure,' said Arthur. 'You keep practising.'

'I will. See you.'

CHAPTER THREE
Only Fools and Family

Orlando got up very early on Sunday morning. It was a special day and he was going to have some fun.

A lot of fun!

He had been planning this for over two weeks, making sure that everything would work. Last night he had been very busy in his room and would not allow anyone to disturb him, especially Sylvester who had become quite angry because of this.

Later, when everyone had gone to bed, he had crept downstairs and prepared a bowl of breakfast cereal for his sister and Sylvester, and put them in the freezer safely out of sight overnight with Tyrone's fruit juice.

*

First thing in the morning, before everybody got up, Orlando dashed to the kitchen and taped a balloon to one of Ma's cooking trays. Then he went to the fridge and took out a can of squirty cream and sprayed the balloon completely. From his pocket, he took out three packets of sprinkles and began the difficult task of covering the cream. He stood back to admire his handy work.

IT LOOKED GOOD.

IT LOOKED LIKE A CAKE.

He placed it into the oven for later. It would look as though it had just been cooked.

Next, he poured warm water into Arthur's empty glue bottle and shook it vigorously to clean it. He smelled it and was satisfied that it had no more glue within. He washed the outside of the container carefully so that he did not spoil the label. It said **Wood Glue** in large letters. It was important for the label to be seen clearly. Then he poured some cream into the bottle and screwed the top back on.

HE LEFT IT ON THE TABLE.

He was really enjoying himself now and he

hummed a little tune, *I Gotta Feeling* by the Black Eyed Peas. As he did so he opened a packet of Oreos and took one out. Cautiously he twisted the biscuit until the top and bottom came apart. Then taking a tube of toothpaste out of his other pocket, he spread some over the creamy centre and stuck the top biscuit back in place. He did exactly the same to the first six biscuits, then carefully positioned them back into the packet.

Hmm, I gotta feeling. This is fun, he thought.

He looked in the freezer and checked the two bowls of cereal. Frozen beautifully! He also checked to see if Tyrone's fruit juice was ready. Frozen beautifully, too. With the straw still in place.

He now set the table with cutlery and, using the little tube of superglue which he had 'borrowed' from Arthur yesterday, he put a tiny spot under the bowl of Sylvester's spoon and placed it back down. He counted ten seconds just like Arthur told him, then tested it. It would not budge. Fantastic!

That today's gonna be... he hummed.

He heard noises from upstairs. Someone was

awake. He needed to move quickly. Otherwise he would miss the fun. From a bag he had placed on the table he took out a handful of small sticky eyes and began placing them in pairs all over everything in the fridge – eggs, milk, sprouts, cartons, cheese, potatoes, **everything!**

He closed the fridge and reopened it to check on the effect. It was superb. A hundred eyes stared back at him.

That today's gonna be a good day...

A SCREAM!

A monster scream smashed through the house, bouncing off walls and filling everywhere with fear.

Then a **BANG!**

Orlando smiled. Channing had just found his little toilet joke.

He flew up the stairs, two at a time, laughing all the way to Channing's room. She was in her en-suite, staring down at her toilet. The face of a vile monster with its tongue hanging out stared up at her!

Channing had her hand over her mouth, the way girls do when they are shocked or frightened, and she was breathing hard. Orlando suppressed a giggle. He had planted the picture there last night. **Result!** This was better than he could *ever* have imagined.

'YOU did this!' she blasted at him.

Orlando burst out laughing, knowing that he had given himself away. Channing leapt at him with a savage rage in her eyes – just as Ma and Tyrone appeared in the bedroom.

'WHAT'S GOING ON IN HERE?!' she roared.

'Look what he's done, Ma!' Channing yelled, refraining from strangling her lunatic brother.

Sylvester came in holding Beyonsay's hand and they all crowded into the en-suite to see.

Ma put her hand to her mouth. 'Ugh, that's not nice!' she said. 'Sylvester, take Beyonsay out. I don't want her to see that picture.'

Reluctantly, Sylvester turned and left.

'Tyrone go and find your teddy.' He did not need to be told twice.

'Orlando, what's this all about?' she said with a fierce look on her face. Then, slowly, she began to realise what was going on, and could not resist a tiny smile. Actually, it was more of a twitch at the corner of her mouth. She did not want Channing to think that she was condoning this prank.

'**April Fools** ' Orlando blurted.

'Oh, it's April Fool's Day, is it?' asked Ma, trying to relieve the tension. 'There's a surprise! Come on, get dressed and go down for breakfast.'

'Good idea, Ma,' Orlando agreed, and went to his own bedroom to wait for the next squeal.

That was brilliant, he thought. *I think I'll put hens and straw in her bed next year!*

He quickly got dressed, sat on his bed, listened and waited. **IT DID NOT TAKE LONG.**

'Ma, what's wrong with these socks? I can't put them on,' Sylvester said with a whine.

Orlando giggled.

'Mine won't go on cither,' shouted Tyrone.

'We can't put our socks on, Ma,' Sylvester and Tyrone shouted together.

Orlando was bent over trying not to laugh out loud.

'You can't get me with that old trick,' Ma shouted back. 'I'm not going to fall for that one!'

'But I can't!' said Sylvester.

'No, I've heard that one before. I'm no April Fool.'

The two boys went into Ma's room where she was changing Beyonsay. 'Look, Ma. Watch.' They sat down on the bed and each tried to put on a sock. They could only push their feet half way and no further. 'See Ma,' said Sylvester.

'That's strange. Let me see.'

They gave the socks to Ma and she could immediately see what was wrong. Someone had put a few stitches of cotton across the ankle part of each sock. 'Now who could have done this?' she asked, looking up to see Orlando standing in the doorway with his arms folded, smiling.

'*April Fools*' he said. '**Gotcha**.' He laughed loudly.

'What is an April Fool, Ma?' asked Tyrone.

'We are,' she responded. 'Orlando has caught us all again.' In spite of herself, she was beginning to be impressed at his resourcefulness.

'What is wrong with these stupid slippers?' Channing yelled and her two slippers flew through the air on to the landing.

'What is the matter now?' Ma called from her room.

'I can't get them on!'

'They can't have shrunk overnight, can they?' Ma asked in a matter of fact way. 'Let me see.' She headed towards Channing's room carrying Beyonsay and stopped at the slippers. She examined them carefully and began to laugh. 'You've been had again!' she told Channing.

'What do you mean?'

'Look. There's tissue paper screwed up in the toe end. No wonder you can't get them on.'

Orlando stood at the top of the stairs with his hand on the bannister, beaming. '**Gotcha!**' was all he said as he disappeared downstairs. Ma laughed and reluctantly, so did Channing.

'How can I get him back, Ma?' asked Channing.

'We'll think of something, don't worry.' Ma smiled and winked. She had something up her sleeve. 'There's plenty of time yet! We have until twelve noon to get our own back.'

Everyone arrived in the kitchen to see that Orlando had laid the table and was pouring juice for everyone.

He had put cereal out already.

'This is very unusual and unexpected, Orlando. *'Why* are you being so helpful?' Channing asked.

'Well it's Sunday. It's special. I've had a bit of fun. We are in our new house and tomorrow we start our new school.'

'You don't like school!' Channing pointed out suspiciously. 'What are you doing now?'

'I thought I'd show you all how thoughtful I can be. That's all. Come on, everyone, enjoy your breakfast.'

Tyrone was the first to **squeal!** He picked up his fruit juice and sucked on the straw. Nothing came out. He sucked again then began to whine. 'I can't drink my juice.'

'Course you can,' said Orlando. 'Suck harder.'

'I have and it won't come out.'

Orlando grabbed the juice from him and pretended to suck the juice so hard that his cheeks sank in and his eyes turned inwards at the corners. **Everyone laughed.**

'Watch this,' said Orlando with a glint in his eye. Slowly he tipped the glass upside down. Tyrone pulled away, expecting the juice to splash everywhere. He yelped and ducked, then slowly turned back.

Nothing came out.

Tyrone looked on in absolute wide-eyed wonder and began to clap. Beyonsay copied him and giggled.

Orlando dropped the frozen juice into a dish, 'Now you can *eat* your juice,' he smiled. 'Oh, and Tyrone?'

'Yes, Orlando.'

'**Gotcha!** Come on everyone, eat your cereal.'

Tyrone, Ma and Channing picked up their spoons and dipped them into their dishes. Sylvester seemed to be having some trouble with his spoon.

'Come on, Sylvester, eat your cereal,' Orlando said in an encouraging tone.

'I'm trying to—'

He was cut short by Channing. *'Aaagh!'* she yelled. *'He's done it again!'* Orlando doubled up laughing.

'What's the matter?' Ma asked.

'Look' My milk is solid! I can't get my spoon into it!'

Sylvester was frustrated. 'I can't pick *my* spoon up!'

Orlando hooted like an owl. *This is the best April Fool's Day I've ever had*, he thought. 'You need more strength, Sylvie!'

'Ma. Tell him! My name is *not* Sylvie!'

'That's correct, Orlando. Stop calling him Sylvie,' she nagged.

'OK, sorry, Sylvester,' he said mockingly. 'Well it's time for my breakfast now.'

He picked up the container of wood glue and poured it all over his cereal. Everyone watched in silence.

He would not dare, thought Channing. 'Go on. I dare you!' she said.

'Don't you dare!' roared Ma. Orlando dipped his spoon into the bowl and ate. '**No!**' shouted Ma.

He dipped in again and ate heartily. 'Umm, this is delicious,' he said rubbing his tummy with his other hand. 'Eat your breakfast, Sylvester,' he encouraged.

'You know I can't pick up my spoon! It's stuck to the table!'

'No way!' said Orlando with a mouthful of cereal.

'*Ha, ha, ha,*' he began to laugh, then looked deadly serious as white liquid oozed from his mouth and slowly ran down his chin.

His eyes opened wide and he clutched his throat with both hands. He forced through his tight lips, 'I... can't... open... my... mouth!' He began to slide to the floor.

Ma was the first to rush to help him. 'Quick,' she said. 'Get some warm water!' Channing grabbed a glass from the draining board as Orlando rolled about. Instantly he looked up at them with a huge grin on his face. 'GOTCHA!'

'Orlando, you had me very worried then,' Ma said, her voice both angry and relieved at the same time. 'Don't ever do anything like that again!'

'I won't, Ma,' he replied. 'Well at least not until next April Fool's Day.'

'Right. Is that it now? Have you **finished**?' she demanded.

'Yes, Ma. I've finished,' he answered. 'And just to prove it, I've made a big cake for us all to enjoy.'

Using oven gloves, he took it out of the oven very

cautiously, making it appear as though it was quite heavy.

Placing it on the table, he stepped back for everyone to admire. Channing was very suspicious, but Sylvester and Tyrone thought it was amazing. Ma just looked on wondering what would happen next.

'Orlando it looks fantastic!' said Sylvester. Tyrone and Beyonsay clapped and cheered.

Orlando beamed. 'Thank you. I just hope it tastes as good as it looks. Sylvester, would you like to cut it?' he said, handing him the knife, giving him no chance to refuse.

'I've never...'

'Oh come on, you're old enough now to cut a cake. Isn't he, Ma?'

Ma was still not sure how this was going to end, so she said hesitantly, 'If he wants to cut it, let him do it. But be very careful, that's all. Hold the knife like this.' She showed him. 'And keep your other hand well out of the way.'

Sylvester took the knife in his hand and prepared to cut into the cake.

'Push the point down into the cake,' Orlando advised, moving around the table to the far side. Sylvester did just that and there was a colossal explosion.

BANG!

Sprinkles and cream flew in all directions. Sylvester was the closest and was covered completely. He looked as though he had a really bad case of measles!

Tyrone, Ma and Channing all looked at each other then started laughing. Beyonsay looked frightenend and began to cry loudly.

Sylvester could not see the funny side and Ma took the knife from him – just in case he forgot it was in his hand! She popped it into the sink and went to soothe Beyonsay. Everyone had sprinkles over their clothes and faces. Ma used her finger to clear some of the cream from Beyonsay's face and pushed it into her mouth. Beyonsay stopped crying.

'You like that, don't you?' she said and scraped some cream from her own face and put it in her own mouth. 'Oh, this is nice!' she said. Beyonsay giggled and put her sprinkle-covered hand into her mouth.

Tyrone copied. 'I like this,' he said and licked some off teddy.

They all tasted the creamy sprinkles. *'This is a new way to eat a cake,'* said Ma and everyone laughed. Even Sylvester.

Twenty minutes later, when the kitchen was clean again, Orlando placed the packet of Oreo biscuits on the table and excused himself. 'I'm going to get cleaned up, Ma,' he announced.

In his room, he waited.

It did not take long.

'Ma, these biscuits taste like toothpaste!' Tyrone shouted.

'What an amazing April Fool's Day,' Orlando said aloud. 'Only the eyes in the fridge now.'

CHAPTER FOUR
Don't Get Mad – Get Even!

Downstairs Ma gave Channing a small piece of paper. 'Can you please take this round to Arthur and Margaret. It's my mobile number. Tell Arthur to ring me, but not to say anything. Tell him that I will do all the talking. Tell him we are trying to April Fool Orlando.'

'What are you going to do, Ma?' asked Channing.

'*Revenge*, Channing. Sweet revenge,' she replied with a smile.

'**Yes-s-s!**' Channing was delighted and clenched her fist.

Ten minutes later she was back and out of breath. 'It's done, Ma. What are you going to do?'

Ma smiled and put her finger to her lips. She sidled into the hall and placed her phone on the table, next to where the flower vase used to be. No sooner had she put it down than it began to ring.

RING! RING! RING!

She let it ring several times before picking it up.

'I'll get it!' Ma called very loudly, so that Orlando would hear in his room.

'Hello... Yes, this is Mrs Shufflett. Who is this?'

'Hello, Becky. This is Arthur.'

'Mrs Chisholm?'

PAUSE.

'No, it's me, Arthur, from next door.'

'Oh yes, Mrs Chisholm from the school.' Ma spoke loudly now. 'You're the Head Teacher, I know. Hello, Mrs Chisholm.'

PAUSE.

Arthur now understood and coughed to indicate his complicity. 'Do you need me to say anything else now, Becky, or shall I stay nice and quiet?'

'Yes, that would be very kind. Yes – they will be

starting tomorrow.'

'I'll just stay quiet,' he said.

Upstairs, Orlando had heard the phone ring and was listening in to Ma's conversation.

'You need them to do what?' Ma asked. 'Do you need this for tomorrow?'

Upstairs Orlando listened intently.

'You *do*. That does not give them much time, does it?' said Ma. 'I will see what I can do.'

'Is it working?' Arthur enquired.

'I don't know yet,' Ma replied. 'I will have to make a note or I shall forget. Can you hold on while I get a piece of paper and a pen?'

'I've got nothing else to do,' said Arthur on the other end of the line.

'Orlando!' Ma shouted. 'Can you bring me a pen and some paper down quickly? It's Mrs Chisholm from the school and I need to write something down.'

Orlando appeared at the top of the stairs with pen and paper in hand. He looked very apprehensive.

'Bring them down – quickly,' Ma badgered. Orlando was perplexed, but brought them down, hesitating after handing them to Ma.

'Thank you, Orlando,' she said, taking them from him. 'You can go now.' Orlando did not want to go. He hung around waiting to hear the rest of the conversation.

'OK, Mrs Chisholm, I'm ready.' She paused a long time.

'Tables 7, 8, 9 and 12. Did you say 12?' Pause. 'Yes I've got that. Is that all?' Another pause.

'How is it going, Becky?' Arthur asked at the other end. Orlando was beginning to look pale.

A long pause then. 'OK, I understand,' said Ma. 'You would like ten words ending in i-o-u-s?'

Pause.

'Yes, I've got that. I've written it down. I think Orlando will be quite bilious when he hears this,' she laughed. 'That's a good i-o-u-s word, isn't it?' She looked at Orlando. He was looking horrified.

Arthur laughed too. 'Sick as a dog!' he added.

'Is there anything else?'

PAUSE.

Orlando looked at Ma with his mouth wide open.

Channing came into the hall from the kitchen.

'A paragraph about their favourite person. It could be from television, films, entertainment or sport. OK, I've got that. I think they will have to start right away or they will not have time to get it finished for tomorrow.'

PAUSE.

Orlando now looked as though he *really was* about to be sick.

'OK, Mrs Chisholm. Thank you.'

PAUSE.

'Yes, thank you. Leave that with me and I will get that done for you. Pardon? Only for Orlando and Channing?'

'What!' Orlando said incredulously. He looked agonisingly at Channing.

'How is Orlando taking it?' Arthur asked on the other end of the line. 'Has he fallen for it?'

'I think so,' Ma replied. 'No problem and thank you for calling. We will see you tomorrow morning, 'Bye.'

'Bye,' said Arthur, laughing loudly. 'I wish I could

see his face now,' and he put the phone down.

Ma looked at the twins. 'That was Mrs Chisholm, the Head Teacher. She wants you two to do some work for tomorrow so that she can assess you.'

Orlando was almost purple.

'What... she can't... but it's Sunday... we should not have to... why? Oh this is *not* fair!'

'It will not take you long if you get started now. It's only eleven o'clock.'

'But I don't see why we should have to—'

'Be quiet, Orlando and listen. Mrs Chisholm wants you both to write out your 7, 8, 9 and 12 times tables and ten words ending in i-o-u-s with their meanings. Then, when you've done that, she wants a paragraph about your favourite person. Understand?'

'I understand, Ma,' Channing said with typical enthusiasm.

'Orlando? Do you understand?'

SILENCE.

'Orlando?'

'Yes, Ma, I understand,' he replied. He felt broken. His wonderful day had just been turned upside down.

Ruined!

'Good. Go and get started now and I will check on you in twenty minutes.'

They went up to their rooms. Channing bounced happily while Orlando trudged.

Thirty minutes later Ma, carrying Beyonsay, looked in on Orlando. 'How are you getting on?' she enquired.

'I've done the tables and six of the spellings,' he muttered.

Channing appeared in the doorway with Sylvester and Tyrone.

'That's very good, Orlando. Very good for an...
APRIL FOOL!' They all shouted it together.

Then, 'GOTCHA!' they exclaimed, and everybody laughed. Even Orlando, although he did roll up the paper and throw it at Channing. Sylvester and Tyrone did high fives and Beyonsay clapped and giggled.

'I did not see *that* coming,' he admitted. 'You're all a bunch of rascals!' He took off down the stairs to the kitchen, determined to have the last April Fools trick of the day. 'I'm hungry. Let's see what is in the fridge.'

'That is a great idea,' Sylvester shouted and ran after him.

'Wait for me,' cried Tyrone, 'I've got to get Teddy.'

When they had all gone, Channing looked at Ma and said, 'Ma, that was brilliant. You're a genius!'

'Oh, I've had a bit of practice over the years. I have to admit though that Orlando really fooled me a few times today. But, it's nearly over now. It's almost twelve o'clock. There's no time for any more April Fool's tricks this year.'

But she spoke too soon.

'Ma!' shouted Tyrone from the bottom of the stairs. 'Ma! Come and see what is in the fridge!'

Ma knew. She had already opened the fridge several times this morning but she did not let on. 'Oh, what can it be?'

The Shufflett family owned four DVDs. That's all. After lunch, and after the usual arguing and fighting over which of the four to watch, everyone sat down in front of the television.

On Ma's instruction, they left the final decision to Beyonsay to avoid any further arguments. 'Pickle,' she gurgled. 'Pickle.'

'Pickle?' Sylvester queried.

'She means *Despicable Me*,' said Channing, and that started the arguing all over again.

'No she does not!'

'Yes, she does!'

'Pickle,' Beyonsay repeated, clapping her hands.

'You're just saying that because *you* want to watch it!' Orlando bawled.

'Pickle me,' said Beyonsay.

'See,' Channing felt vindicated. 'Pickle me – *Despicable Me*.'

That seemed to settle it. 'Beyonsay is beginning to talk properly now,' Ma said proudly.

Ma had decided that they would all sit down to enjoy the film together as a family.

'Well not quite a family,' said Orlando. 'Dad's not here.'

'When is he coming home, Ma?' the children all said at once.

'I don't know exactly,' Ma responded, 'but it will not be too long.'

'How long is that?' Orlando persisted.

'Look,' said Ma slightly irritably, 'can we watch the film in peace?'

The three boys sat together on the sofa and Channing sat with Beyonsay on her lap on the armchair. Ma tidied up around them.

After twenty minutes, Beyonsay had had enough of Pickle Me. She slid off Channing's lap and **dropped** to the floor. She crawled to the dresser and opened a door. The dresser was full of games and toys. She sifted through them, picking up one after another only to drop them on to the floor.

Tyrone spotted the *Gruffalo* jigsaw and joined Beyonsay. He knelt down to do the jigsaw while Beyonsay found a box of beads. The sort you can make into a necklace or wrist band.

Tyrone finished his jigsaw and began to help his little sister sort out the beautiful coloured beads. The older three children were engrossed in the film. He helped her to thread them on to a long string. Beyonsay put it over her head as a necklace, but the string was not tied, so the beads slithered off and bounced and rolled everywhere. Tyrone laughed and began to gather them up. With shock, he noticed that Beyonsay had a bead in her ear! As he moved to get a closer look, she pushed another bead up her **nose!**

'Nose,' she giggled.

Tyrone thought this was very funny and began to laugh.

By this time, Ma was in the kitchen. Tyrone ran to her. 'Ma, Bee has a bead up her nose and one in her ear.'

Ma broke into laughter and Tyrone laughed too.

'That's a really good trick, but it's after twelve o'clock and you can't do April Fools after twelve o'clock.'

Tyrone looked bewildered. 'She *really* has got a bead up her nose.' He repeated, 'and one in her ear.'

Ma looked at him in dismay, trying to work out if he was trying a trick on her. Then they both burst out laughing again and Sylvester came in to find out what was going on.

'Sylvester, will you go and have a look please?' Ma took off her pink gloves and the smile became a little bit uneasy. She was becoming doubtful and worried.

Sylvester came **racing** back in. 'She has a bead up her nose and one in her ear!'

Ma put her hand to her mouth and followed him back into the lounge. Channing was already trying to get the bead out of her ear.

'No! Stop!' Ma cried. 'You might push it further in. Let me see.'

Beyonsay had one hand on her ear and the other was placed delicately on her nose. 'Nose,' she giggled looking up at Ma. 'Nose.'

Ma looked down at her and felt helpless.

CHAPTER FIVE
Don't Go Breaking My Chair!

After a few minutes of trying to remove the two beads, Ma had to admit defeat.

'We've got to get her to hospital,' she announced. 'Channing, ring Margaret. She'll know what to do.' Ma handed her mobile to Channing.

Arthur answered. 'Hello,' he said cheerfully.

'Hello, Arthur. This is Channing from next door. Can Ma speak to Margaret please?'

'I'm sorry but Margaret is out. She works at the hospital on a Sunday afternoon.'

Channing gave the phone to Ma.

'Hello, Arthur. I have a little problem with Beyonsay. She's pushed a bead up her nose and another in her ear. I'm very worried because I can't get them out. I think we need to get her to the hospital.'

'Oh dear!' he said. 'Look, don't worry. I will drive you there. Just give me a few minutes and I'll come and collect you.'

They all put on their coats and shoes and were waiting at the front door when Arthur drove up a few minutes later. He looked rather concerned when he saw them all standing there waiting. 'Oh dear,' he muttered. 'There's six of you, plus me, that's seven and my car only has five seats. I'm not sure how we can all fit in.'

Ma was in no mood for any more problems. She had a very determined look on her face.

ALMOST SCARY.

'The Bab will sit on my lap in the back,' she thundered, 'with Sylvester and Channing. Tyrone can sit on Orlando's lap in the front. Right, everybody – move!'

'And Teddy can sit on *my* lap,' smiled Tyrone, looking very pleased.

'I'm not sure that Tyrone would be allowed to sit on anyone's lap in the front. I think it is against the law,' Arthur said, trying to dissuade Ma.

'Arthur, this is an *emergency*! I'm sure that PC Plod will understand on this occasion. Please can we get going?'

Arthur could see that it was no use trying to argue with Ma. She was a determined woman and she had made up her mind. With a shrug of his shoulders, Arthur ensured that everyone had their seat belts safely fixed before setting off.

Twenty minutes later, he pulled up at the Community Hospital.

In the little café just inside the main doors, Margaret was pouring a cup of tea for a customer from a large, old-fashioned, metal teapot. She looked up to see Ma, carrying Beyonsay, bustling through the hospital reception hall, followed by Channing and Sylvester.

That's very strange, she thought.

Arthur came **bursting** through next with Orlando and Tyrone. Just at the wrong moment, Tyrone dropped Teddy and they waited impatiently while he went back to pick it up, then hurried after the others.

Margaret's face was a picture of bewilderment.

'Margaret!' a loud voice called to her. 'Margaret, look what you are doing!' Margaret was still pouring the tea and the cup was now overflowing. The saucer was overflowing. There was tea all over the counter and a small waterfall was sloshing to the floor. Margaret was horrified and quickly stopped pouring.

'Oh my goodness!' she cried. 'What a mess! I'm so sorry!' She put the kettle down and reached for a large tea towel. 'Oh dear, oh dear, oh dear!' She was completely **flummoxed**. 'Everywhere I go those kids next door seem to follow me!'

'Pardon,' said her friend, Deirdre, who was now helping to mop up the tea.

'Those kids next door! They are a menace!'

'I'm not sure I understand what you mean, Margaret,' Deirdre said kindly.

'Those children who just went through reception. They are my next door neighbours. The ones I was telling you about. The ones who catapulted sprouts at us. *Those kids next door!'*

Ma had arrived at the reception desk. There was a

name plate which said:

Mrs Grunge did not appear to be very welcoming. She was an elderly, stern-looking lady who continued to look down and write. Orlando noticed that she had a hairy mole on her chin and began to chuckle. He nudged Sylvester and pointed. 'Witch,' he whispered. Sylvester snorted as he tried to stifle a laugh.

Ma was impatient and coughed politely. The lady continued her writing. Ma was decidedly unimpressed and the children knew what was coming next.

'Excuse me!' Ma barked.

The lady stopped writing and slowly looked up at Ma with laser-like eyes.

This is a battle I would love *to fight on another day,* Ma thought. *But today is not the day.* So she spoke very softly, in a whisper. 'Hello, Matilda, I'm terribly sorry to interrupt your very important work.' Matilda had to lean forward to hear what Ma was saying.

Good, you little rat! Ma thought. *Now I've got your attention.* She continued to whisper. 'So, please excuse our intrusion but we have a slight emergency here with my little baby. I'm sure you can help us.'

Matilda softened. 'Oh dear, what seems to be the matter?'

Gotcha! Ma thought. Then, very gently she said, 'Beyonsay has pushed a bead up her nose and another in her ear and I cannot get them out.'

'Oh dear! That sounds quite worrying,' Matilda replied.

'Yes it does, doesn't it?' Ma agreed.

'I'm very sorry,' Matilda continued, 'but we haven't got an A and E here.'

'A what?' Ma asked.

'An A and E. An Accident and Emergency department.'

'Well this is a hospital, isn't it?' Ma could feel her irritation level going up again.

'Yes,' replied Matilda getting to her feet. 'But, don't worry, I will have a word to see if one of the doctors can come and have a look at her.'

Ma's irritation level went down again.

'Please take a seat.' Matilda indicated to the waiting area. 'I will be back in a moment.'

They all marched over to the seats just as Margaret arrived. 'What's the matter?' she enquired looking very worried.

Ma and Arthur explained and Margaret sat down to wait with them.

Two minutes later Orlando and Sylvester were bored. Orlando Swung his feet back and forth making a scuffing noise on the floor. Sylvester joined in.

'Stop it you two and sit still!' Ma ordered.

'I spy with my little eye, something beginning with "b".' Channing began the game.

'I know!' shouted Tyrone. 'Bee!'

'Nearly,' she responded quite impressed with his answer.

'Beyonsay,' Sylvester added triumphantly.

'No,' she said.

'It is. I can tell. You are changing it because you don't want to lose!' Sylvester was adamant he was correct.

'Keep your voice down, Sylvester. We don't want to be thrown out of here,' Ma scolded.

'I got it right, Ma. Channing is cheating now.'

'You did not get it right, Sylvester,' Channing countered. It's *not* Beyonsay. It's something *on* Beyonsay. Or should I say *in* Beyonsay?'

For the first time, Orlando joined in. '*In* Beyonsay?' he asked. 'Is it *in* her ear?'

Channing smirked.

'Bead!' they all called out together.

'Right. That's enough now. You're too noisy,' Ma

insisted. 'End of game!'

A man in a white coat appeared through a doorway. He had a stethoscope around his neck. 'Hello. Are you the lady with the bead problem?' He was friendly and smiled at them.

'Yes. Well, my baby has the problem,' Ma clarified, smiling back. 'Are you the doctor?'

'Yes, I'm Doctor Dean,' he replied.

'Is that your first name or your last name?' Orlando queried.

'Orlando!' Ma gave him the look. 'Don't be so cheeky.'

The doctor laughed. 'It's a good question.'

'Yes. It could be either,' Orlando explained.

'It's my surname. Does that make a difference?'

'No. I just wondered that's all,' and Orlando laughed with the doctor.

'Now let me see,' he said looking in Beyonsay's ear and nose. 'Hmm. Yes. They do seem to be stuck, don't they? You're supposed to wear your jewellery on the *outside*, young lady,' he said smiling at Beyonsay. 'Now, what's your name?' he asked the Bab, tickling her chin.

'It's Beyonsay.' Ma looked at him with a worried expression.

'Aah – my favourite singer. Don't worry,' he said. 'This is something we can sort out quite quickly. Some olive oil in both will make it easier for them to slide out, then we will use suction to remove them. Could you bring her into the cubicle over there for me?'

'Can I come with you?' asked Channing.

'And me!' Tyrone said with a GURGLE.

'Yes, of course. You can all come in if you want.'

'I think I will stay out here and read a magazine,' said Orlando

'I'll stay with Orlando,' Sylvester said.

They all disappeared into the cubicle.

'Well, let's go and have a nice cup of tea, shall we?' Arthur asked. 'There's nothing we can do for the moment.'

Margaret thought that was a good idea, but the boys declined. Arthur and Margaret disappeared to the café.

Orlando sat for exactly ten seconds before PUSHING his chair backwards to slide along the polished floor.

Sylvester watched as Orlando spun around and slid back.

He turned his chair around again and looked at Sylvester with a gleam in his eye. 'Bet I can slide the furthest with one shove,' he challenged.

'We will see about that,' Sylvester responded.

'Ready?' Orlando took charge. 'Set... **GO!**' They both pushed as hard as they could, their chairs sliding backwards. Orlando won by almost half a metre. They turned around and levelled up for the next shove.

'I'll say go this time,' Sylvester demanded.

'One, two, three, **GO!**' They shoved as hard as they could manage and Orlando won again.

'I know,' he said. 'You start over there and I'll start over here and we can play bumper cars!'

They moved into position and had their backs to each other. 'Are you ready, Sylvia?' Orlando said, tormenting his brother.

'I'll get you for that!' Sylvester roared back.

'Three, two, one, GO!' They both took off like Formula One cars. They met in the middle with a resounding CRUNCH!

The back leg of Orlando's chair buckled and folded like a piece of wet cardboard and Orlando went sprawling. He got up immediately, laughing like a hyena. 'That was amazing!' he **boomed.**

Sylvester laughed too. He stood with both arms raised aloft in victorious salute just like Lewis Hamilton.

But they both spotted the damaged chair at the same time.

'Oops! Quick, let's hide it behind all the other chairs,' Orlando said with a whisper.

Before they had a chance to hide the evidence, they heard Ma coming back into the waiting room with Beyonsay and the others.

Orlando grabbed a magazine and swiftly moved to another seat with Sylvester next to him. They began to look at the magazine together, looking quite shifty.

Orlando looked up, 'Oh, hello.' He smiled his sickliest smile. 'Is everything all right now?'

Ma looked less worried. 'Well, the doctor has put warm oil in her ear and up her nose to help the beads to come out. We need to wait for a few minutes to see if the beads free themselves naturally.'

'What happens if they don't fall out naturally, Ma?' Orlando asked.

'In that case, he will use a suction machine.'

'Ooh, will it hurt?' asked Sylvester.

'He said it will not hurt at all but it makes a bit of a hissing noise, so the Bab might be frightened.'

'The wheels on the bus go round and round,' Channing sang and Beyonsay joined in with the actions.

A huge man in a brown coat, carrying a bulging black bin liner, walked past and noticed the damaged chair. He stopped and walked over to pick it up. He studied it with great care, frowning, turning it around to examine it from different angles. He did *not* look pleased and heaved a **LOUD** angry sigh. Slowly, he looked around the waiting room then, eventually, he turned his gaze to the two boys. They slid down behind the magazine and looked at each other. Worried, they held their breath.

After what seemed like forever, the man picked up the black bag and turned to go. Orlando could not resist a quick look at him. He peeked over the magazine and, to his horror, the man was still looking at him! He ducked down again and the man disappeared down a corridor.

'*The wipers on the bus went swish, swish, swish,*' Channing sang and Beyonsay waved her arms excitedly.

Orlando was worried and searched for a way to break the tension of their lucky escape. 'I need the loo, Ma,' he announced. 'Where is it?'

Ma looked around and pointed to a sign. 'Through those doors over there,' she said. 'Don't be long and don't get into trouble.'

'Of course not, Ma,' he retorted. 'How could I in here?'

He did not have long to wait!

Orlando went through the doors and turned down a corridor. He walked past several curtained off areas and was just about to peek behind one of the curtains when. . .

'Excuse me, young man. Can I have a word?'

Orlando spun around to see the man in the brown coat standing at the end of the curtains. He gulped and stared in fear. The man said nothing, just silently

76

beckoned with his finger for Orlando to go to him.

Like a moth to a candle, Orlando felt himself dragged by an invisible force towards the man who held open the curtain and, as he approached, Orlando could see a table inside and lying on the table was a broken chair.

The broken chair!

The man ushered him in and said, 'Sit down, young sir, and tell me what you know about this.'

Back in the waiting room, Sylvester was also getting bored and decided to go looking for Orlando. 'I need the loo as well,' he said.

'Don't be long and don't go messing about!' Ma insisted.

'Of course not, Ma,' he said with a grin, then went through the double swing doors, and as he passed a curtained-off cubicle he heard Orlando's voice coming from behind the curtain.

'Is it broken?' Orlando asked.

A man spoke, 'Yes, it's definitely broken. See? It's broken here at the top and it's badly bent here. Did it hurt when this happened?'

'No, not much.'

Sylvester froze as he heard the man continue, 'You did this skidding across the room, didn't you? Did you fall off the chair?'

Orlando nodded. 'Yes, it tipped over.'

'Did you bang your head?' the man asked.

'No. I bumped my elbow but that doesn't hurt now.'

Sylvester thought about pulling the curtain open.

'So, your elbow is OK, but this *leg* is going to have to come off ,' the man continued.

Sylvester was horrified. He stared at the curtain. 'Orlando's leg is going to have to come off!' he muttered to himself.

'I'm going to have to take this off right now,' said the man. ***The whole leg has got to go.***'

Sylvester 𝔣𝔯𝔬𝔷𝔢 𝔰𝔬𝔩𝔦𝔡!

We might be able to fix a wooden one in its place, but it will not be the same again. Do you understand?'

Orlando mumbled, 'Umm.'

Sylvester sucked air in noisily and put his hand to his mouth. 'Orlando is going to have a wooden leg!'

he hissed. 'How is he going to climb trees?'

'The leg will never be as strong again and it certainly won't look very good. What have you got to say for yourself?'

Sylvester could take no more. He ran.

'Maaaaaa**aaaaa!**'

He yelled all the way down the corridor and through the double doors.

Twenty minutes later, everyone was laughing heartily. The man in the brown coat was laughing. Ma was laughing, and Beyonsay was positively gurgling and clapping her hands. Doctor Dean was laughing and holding the two beads securely in his hand.

Arthur and Margaret had returned and they joined in the merriment.

Only Sylvester was not laughing.

He looked sheepish and sat silently looking at the others enjoying a good laugh.

'Then I said, "This leg has got to come off!"' said

the man in the brown coat.

Everybody laughed once more.

What a noise!

People were coming from all over the hospital to find out what all the fuss was about.

Sylvester tried a smile but it did not really work so he shuffled his feet and asked. 'Can we go home now, Ma?'

They all laughed again!

Grown-ups, Sylvester thought. *I will never understand them as long as I live.*

An hour later they were watching the rest of *Pickle Me* while Ma prepared dinner.

CHAPTER SIX
Rainy Days and Mondays
Always Get me Down

'**M**ove it, you lot. It's half past seven. Breakfast is on the table and school starts in ninety minutes. And we've got to get there yet!' Ma did not like to be kept waiting.

Orlando opened his eyes and realised that this was their first school day since moving house – the first day at their new school. He also remembered that he was not sharing a room with his two brothers. He had no one to throw his pillow at!

That's a bit boring, he thought. So he went into their room and grabbed Tyrone's pillow.

Tyrone woke with a **shriek** as his head banged down onto the mattress. Sylvester woke with a start, spotted Orlando, grabbed his own pillow and so began an epic pillow fight.

The two boys were having a superb time ducking, diving and belting each other, with Tyrone laughing and shouting at them, until Ma appeared at the door.

The fight broke up immediately.

'Tyrone, let me help you with your pillow,' said Orlando, exaggeratedly smoothing Tyrone's pillow back into place. 'There, that looks much better now,' he added.

He looked at Sylvester. 'I say, old bean, would you like me to help you too?'

'Orlando!' roared Ma. 'Don't push your luck. Now, move yourself. All of you get downstairs and eat your breakfast.'

'Yes, Ma!' Orlando said, saluting.

Sylvester and Tyrone copied. 'Yes, Ma!' They all laughed, including Ma.

Orlando had often pictured a wonderful life for himself, with **no** *school,* **no** *homework,* **no** *spellings and* **not** *being forced to learn stuff that did not interest him.* He was fine with dinosaurs and space exploration. He actually enjoyed Maths and Science too, but he could not stand Literacy. There was far too much writing to do, and he could not understand why, when he had read a book, he had to write about it. What was the point in that? He thought that you either enjoyed the story or you didn't.

But today, as he ate his breakfast and listened to the excited chatter of the others, he found, to his surprise, that he did not actually mind having to go to school today.

This also came as a shock to him!

He couldn't quite understand why he wasn't peeved at the prospect of going to school like he used to be.

Well, for one thing, he liked their new house and he had never liked any of their other houses. This house was massive and he had his **own** room. How good was that?

And yesterday had been great fun.

There seemed to be lots to do in the countryside and, finally, going to school on a bus seemed a bit wicked.

He did not know it but, within one hour, he would be whinging and moaning about having to go to school in the countryside!

After breakfast Ma sent the children back to their rooms to wash, do their teeth and to change out of pyjamas into clothes.

Sylvester and Tyrone left the bathroom together and went to their room to get dressed. Just as Sylvester was taking off his pyjama bottoms, Tyrone pushed him off balance. For a few seconds Sylvester lay stark naked on the floor, before leaping up to push Tyrone over.

Ma arrived at the door to see the two boys wearing absolutely **nothing** but a smile. THEY WERE STARKERS!

'Oh my goodness!' she wailed. 'That's not a pretty sight! Pack it in you two and get your pants on! I'll be back in two minutes.'

Two minutes later Ma, thinking that it was very quiet in their room, went back to see how they were getting on.

She entered to see both boys still undressed, except for their underpants but they were not wearing them where they should be. They were both wearing them *on their heads.* They were standing by their beds with their hands to their foreheads, saluting.

Ma laughed hysterically.

'You told us to get our pants on, but you did not tell us where to put them,' Sylvester explained, giggling.

They all laughed again.

This was one of those moments when Ma thought

about taking a photo on her phone. Then she decided against it.

'OK, let's get you dressed before we are all late for school,' she said and began to help Tyrone into his clothes.

Twenty minutes later they were all at the front door, ready to set off down the lane to the bus stop. They had walked about two hundred metres when they passed a wide, five bar gate. It was closed and a large, old house stood in the grounds.

There was no one to be seen.

'That looks haunted to me,' Orlando said. He was staring at the house with a huge grin on his face. He opened his eyes wide and pulled a creepy face.

TYRONE HID BEHIND HIS TEDDY.

'Stop it, Orlando, you're frightening him,' Channing said. 'It does not look anything of the sort. That's a nice house isn't it, Tyrone?'

He peeped out to take a look. 'It's not haunted, Orlando,' he shouted.

'How do you know, my little friend?' He made a

horrible laughing noise like they do in the films. 'Huh, huh, ho, ho, ho-o-o-o!'

Tyrone grabbed Channing's hand.

'That's enough,' murmured Ma. 'You're frightening him and we need to go. We don't want to miss the bus.'

After a short distance, they came to another gate. In the field, a horse trotted up to them and lifted its head over the top rail and snorted.

'Oh look, Beyonsay. It's a horse,' Channing said. 'What do horses do?'

Beyonsay smiled, then squealed, 'Neigh, neigh!'

And everybody laughed and joined in.

'Horses like apples, don't they?' Sylvester asked, taking an apple from his school bag.

'No!' boomed Ma, but it was too late.

Sylvester held up his hand with the apple cupped in his palm and the horse gently took it, leaving splother in its place. UGH!

Orlando laughed as Sylvester gabbled and then it began to rain. Slowly at first. Ma hurriedly put up the hood of the pushchair and opened her umbrella. 'Quickly, put your hoods up,' she encouraged the children.

Channing lifted her hood and helped Tyrone with his. Sylvester did not need to be told twice, but Orlando did not have a hood on his coat.

'Orlando, come under the umbrella with me,' Ma insisted.

He looked up at the darkening sky, squinting against the raindrops, and decided that Ma had made a very good suggestion. He took hold of the pushchair handle next to Ma and they began to walk on down the lane.

There was nothing to see on either side of the lane, except for tall hedgerows of hawthorn bushes. Orlando looked at them remembering the prickly pain of going through one only three days ago.

Water dripped off the umbrella and trickled down his neck.

Cold!

'UGH!'

He tried to move fully under the umbrella, but only

succeeded in tripping over his feet and stepped in a puddle, which splashed Ma's legs as well as his own.

'Ugh, Orlando. Please be careful,' she complained.

'Sorry, Ma,' he replied, stepping in another puddle. He felt cold water soak into his socks.

'This is awful,' he muttered.

Then the rain came down harder. It was beginning to soak through their coats.

'Ma, I'm getting wet!' shrieked Tyrone.

'And me,' Sylvester added, keeping his head down and bending forward.

Water poured off the umbrella and down Orlando's neck again. 'Aagh!' he screamed.

'How much further, Ma?' Channing asked, trying to raise some hope.

'I have no idea,' Ma answered. 'Mr Scroggs said the bus stop was just down the lane.'

She looked ahead but all she could see was *the lane*. She felt very dejected.

Beyonsay began to cry and Ma stopped to care for her. She gave the umbrella to Orlando while she tucked

Beyonsay further inside the hood. Orlando held the brolly over Ma and felt the cold rain on his face and head. *It's just like having a shower,* he thought. *A cold shower!* His hair was now flat to his head and water ran through it and down his face and neck.

He shivered. 'Ma, I'm cold and wet through,' he moaned.

'It shouldn't be long now, son,' she said encouragingly.

But it was.

They went around the next bend to see... another bend.

THEN ANOTHER!

AND

ANOTHER!

AND

ANOTHER!

'I'm freezing cold and wet,' said Sylvester.

'Me too,' Channing added. 'Tyrone is crying, Ma.'

'This is awful!' Orlando wailed. 'I *hate* it. Why can't the bus come to collect us? Why do we have to go to school anyway?'

'This is the worst place yet,' Sylvester moaned.

The rain began to ease a little as they came around the next bend. This time they could see the bus stop and the big red telephone box next to it.

They all cheered.

The amazing thing about the bus stop was that it was a large wooden shelter with a long seat inside.

Channing, Tyrone and Sylvester made a run for it, splashing in several puddles on the way. 'Sorry, Ma,' Channing shouted.

Ma and Orlando arrived to find all three of them breathless, sitting down in the dry.

'Well that was fun wasn't it?' Ma said, trying to cheer them all up.

'**NO!**' they all yelled back.

Ma took out some tissues for them to dry their faces. Tyrone had stopped crying now and looked a little more cheerful as he snuggled up to Channing, but he was dithering.

They sat and watched the rain outside, waiting for the bus to arrive.

They were all feeling miserable.

A man appeared around the side of the shelter. He was carrying a huge umbrella. 'Hello,' he said in a cheery voice. 'I saw you all run into the bus shelter from my house, just behind here. Oh my gosh, you are all soaking wet through.'

'We'll be OK, thanks,' said Ma. 'It should be warm on the bus.'

'I see,' he replied. 'Are you waiting for the bus?'

'Yes,' Ma responded. 'It should be here any minute.'

'Oh dear, no! I'm sorry to say that the next one is not due until eleven o'clock.'

'We are waiting for the *school* bus,' she pointed out.

'I'm afraid you've missed it. It left half an hour ago.'

'No,' said Ma, patiently. 'It doesn't leave until twenty past eight.'

'Yes, that's correct,' he said. 'It's ten to nine now!' It rained all the way back home but Channing, Sylvester and Tyrone were kept reasonably dry under the umbrella lent to them by Arnold Beasley, the kind man. Ma and Orlando sheltered under Ma's brolly.

This was not quite how they had expected their first day at school to be.

Back home everyone changed into dry clothes while Ma rang the school.

'Hello, this is Mrs Shufflett.'

'Oh hello, Mrs Shufflett. We were expecting your children in school today,' said the voice at the other end.

'Yes, I know. I'm sorry but we got soaked in the

rain and missed the bus,' Ma explained.

'I am sorry to hear that, Mrs Shufflett. Please hold the line while I transfer you to Mrs Chisholm, the head teacher.'

THERE WAS A LONG PAUSE AND A CLICK.

'Hello, Mrs Shufflett. This is Mrs Chisholm speaking. I hear you have had a disastrous morning.'

'Yes, we were soaked and missed the school bus,' Ma replied.

'Oh dear, I am so sorry to hear that, but don't worry, we are coming to collect the children. Our caretaker, Mr Carbuncle is just about to set off. He will be with you in about twenty minutes.'

'Thank you, Mrs Chisholm, but I was hoping to come myself today to see the children settle into their new school on their first day.'

'That is no problem,' she replied. 'Alfred has a seven-seater, so he will be able to get you all in.'

'That's very kind, Mrs Chisholm. Do you think he will be able to bring me back home afterwards?'

'Yes, I'm sure he can, but please don't expect this

door to door service every day, will you?' Mrs Chisholm said laughing.

'I won't,' said Ma. 'Thank you so much.'

'We will see you soon, Mrs Shufflett. Goodbye.'

'Goodbye,' said Ma.

The children gathered around and Channing asked, 'Well, Ma, what's happening?'

'We are going to be chauffeur driven to school!' she announced excitedly.

CHAPTER SEVEN
Alice Springs and Birminum

A large car pulled up outside Budleigh Cottage. Then a tall man got out and rang the bell. Everyone was ready and waiting in the hall as Ma opened the door.

Alfred Carbuncle stood looking at them through glasses that were so thick his eyes appeared like conkers.

Orlando immediately burst out laughing and Sylvester tried unsuccessfully to stifle his laugh. It blurted out like a fart. This made everyone else laugh, including Ma who became very embarrassed and said, 'Hello, you must be Mr Conker.'

'Pardon?' said Mr Carbuncle.

Orlando laughed even more.

'Mr Conker,' Ma repeated.

'Carbuncle,' said Alfred.

'Carbuncle?' Ma queried. 'Oh yes, Mr *Carbuncle.*' She could not take her eyes off his glasses.

Orlando was doubled up with laughter. Sylvester too. Even Channing could not hide a giggle.

Orlando muttered to Sylvester, 'I bet he can't find his way back to the car!'

Sylvester snorted another fart again.

'Yes, that's right. You must be Mrs Shufflett,' he responded with a very strong Yorkshire accent.

'Yes,' said Ma, 'and these are my little conkers.'

Orlando **hooted** like an owl.

'Pardon?'

'Children,' Ma corrected herself. 'These are my *children*,' she added, stifling another outburst.

'If he is going to drive us, I'm going to walk in front of the car with a **red flag**!' Channing muttered to Orlando who was now convulsed on his back on the floor, behaving like a dying fly.

'Pack it in, you two,' Ma pleaded, eyes wide and staring, smothering another laugh with great difficulty.

'OK, if everyone is ready, let's get going,' Alfred Carbuncle said.

'They are like two magnifying glasses,' Orlando whispered, climbing to his feet. 'If the sun comes out he will burn to a frazzle!'

'Or start a fire,' Sylvester joined in.

'Get him away from the house quick!'

Alfred led the way to the car and opened one of the rear doors. 'I have got a proper baby seat for your little one,' he pointed out with pride. 'It's for my grand-daughter. She is about the same age.'

'Thank you,' Ma said, as she strapped Beyonsay into the seat and climbed in next to her. 'Your *first* time in a *car*, baby,' Ma said gently to her.

'First time? Surely not,' Alfred Carbuncle queried.

'Yes,' Ma answered. 'We haven't had a car since my husband went to—' She stopped. '...Went to ... erm, join the SAS.'

'The *SAS*?' said Alfred suddenly standing to attention. He lifted his right foot and brought it down hard on the floor, **saluting** with his right hand. 'I was in the Commandos myself Ma'am. Proud of it too!

Sergeant. Eight years.'

'**Wow!**' yelled Orlando suddenly interested. 'Do you mean you were a soldier?'

'Yes, sir,' he replied. 'Covert operations. Far East.'

'*Wow,*' Orlando repeated. 'Did you kill anyone?'

'Orlando! That's enough!' Ma reprimanded him. 'Get in the car.'

'I'm in the front seat,' Orlando called out. 'After all, I'm the eldest.'

Channing mimicked his words as she got into the car next to Ma.

'I'm the eldest! Ner, ner, nu ner, ner!'

Mr Carbuncle opened the door at the back and Tyrone climbed in with Sylvester.

Seventeen minutes later, they were climbing out and stepping onto the car park of their new school.

'Well, this is it,' Mr Carbuncle announced with some pride. 'What do you think?'

'Gosh, it looks lovely,' said Channing. 'It's a lot smaller than some of our other schools, but I like it.'

'What do *you* think, Tyrone?' she asked.

Tyrone looked at Teddy. 'Teddy likes it,' he said with a smile.

Channing smiled back. 'Let's hope we can stay here long enough for me to make some friends this time!' She glowered at Orlando and Sylvester.

Alfred Carbuncle noticed the look and said, 'Oh yes, I am quite sure the boys will love it here. Everyone is very friendly.'

Ma put Beyonsay into the pushchair and Alfred, the caretaker, led the way to the office.

They were met by a very cheery Mrs Gimple, the School Secretary. 'Good morning, Mrs Shufflett. Good morning, children,' she said, sliding open the glass window. Mrs Gimple spoke **very** fast.

Before they had a chance to answer, she continued, 'You finally made it. What a dreadful start to the day for you all. I'm so sorry. But you're here now, safe and sound. Would you sign the book for me please, Mrs Shufflett? I will go and let Mrs Chisholm know that you are here.'

Before Ma could respond, Mrs Gimple had disappeared.

'Well, I've got work to do so, please excuse me.' Mr Carbuncle smiled and turned to leave.

'Thank you, so much,' said Ma. She looked at the children and indicated they should do the same.

'Thank you,' they all said. Ma likes well-mannered children.

So did Mr Carbuncle, 'Oh, don't mention it. It was my pleasure for such a lovely family.'

Ma purred with pride.

Orlando looked around at the artwork on the walls.

A TROPHY CABINET HELD AROUND TEN CUPS AND SHIELDS.

There was a large photograph of the whole school, with all the teachers and other staff. Everyone was smiling on it except for one boy right at the back, who had his back turned to the camera! *I've* **got** *to meet him,* thought Orlando. He grinned and went to have a closer look, but a door suddenly opened and out stepped Mrs Chisholm.

'Good morning, Mrs Shufflett, good morning, children,' she beamed.

She was not very **tall** but, as far as Orlando was concerned, she looked like a typical teacher, with thin glasses on the end of her nose and a bob of hair on the top of her head.

Orlando did not know how old she was but it was obvious that she was older than Ma, so she must be **very** old! She wore a dark striped suit and held her hand out as she walked towards Ma. She looked deadly serious, not at all fun!

There's no way **I'm** *shaking her hand*, he thought.

'I'm very pleased to meet you,' Mrs Chisholm said,

shaking Ma's hand. 'And your lovely children.' *That will soon change,* Channing thought.

'I'm sorry you've had a difficult start to your day. How awful for you all.'

'It's the first time we have walked down the lane, so we did not know how long it would take. We will allow more time tomorrow,' Ma answered. 'The rain made it worse.'

'And the horse,' said Tyrone. 'We stopped to feed the horse in the field. We are going to bring some more apples tomorrow,' he added with some self-satisfaction.

MA LOOKED LIKE A CHILD THAT HAD BEEN CAUGHT RED-HANDED.

Orlando was impressed, thinking that this was the longest he had ever heard Tyrone speak.

'And the haunted h...' Tyrone tried to continue.

'Thank you, Tyrone.' Ma cut him off sharply. 'Mrs Chisholm doesn't want to hear about our problems this morning, does she?'

'He's quite a chatterbox, isn't he?' asked Mrs Chisholm.

Not when you get to know him, Orlando thought. 'We

can't normally get a word out of him!' he said.

'Now, it's time for the children to go to their classrooms and meet their new classmates,' Mrs Chisholm said. She led the way down a short corridor and stopped at a door with a sign which read:

Class 6H
Miss Hanlon

WE CELEBRATE HARD WORK AND EFFORT AS MUCH AS SUCCESS.

Mrs Chisholm knocked the door and walked in. Miss Hanlon was sitting with a group of children and looked up.

'Good morning, Miss Hanlon. Good morning, Class 6H.'

Like a drone, the children **CHANTED** out, 'Good morning, Mrs Chisholm. Good morning, everyone.'

'It looks as though you are all working very hard. May we come in?'

I bet nobody says no, Orlando thought.

Mrs Chisholm waited for the whole family to enter the room, then announced them to the children.

'Children, this is the newest family to join our school. They have come from a big city far away in England. I know you are going to make them welcome and help them to settle into our school, aren't you?'

A few children answered, 'Yes, Mrs Chisholm.'

'Good.' She turned to the children. 'Why don't you introduce yourselves, so that we all know who you are?' She pointed to Channing.

'Hi, my name is Channing and I'm a twin.' Channing looked confident and assertive. She did not want anyone to think she was a pushover.

'Good girl, Channing,' said Mrs Chisholm and pointed at Orlando.

'Hi. I'm Orlando and Channing is my twin sister. I'm the eldest.' He could not resist letting them know. Channing avoided his eyes.

'Now I'm quite sure Miss Hanlon has told you that they are joining Class 6H and I want you to make sure that they are not left alone at playtimes.'

'Yes, that's correct,' said Miss Hanlon. 'We have

already discussed who will be playing with them every day this week. We want them to meet everyone.'

She looks really nice, Channing thought. *I like her.*

She's very pretty, thought Orlando.

'Very good, 6H. I know I can rely on you. Now for the rest of the family.' She pointed to Sylvester.

'My name is Sylvester and I like cricket.'

'Sylvester will be joining Class 4G,' Mrs Chisholm added. 'And now, this young man here.' She pointed at Tyrone and he **squirmed** behind Ma to avoid the gaze from five million children! **TEN MILLION EYES!**

Several of the children said 'Aah,' and laughed which made Tyrone go red.

'This is Tyrone and he is quite shy,' said Ma coming to his rescue.

'Treat him kindly children,' Mrs Chisholm stressed. 'He is going into Reception Class with Mrs Norbury and Miss Dabney. And this is Mrs Shufflett and baby Beyonsay, who is a bit too young to come to school yet!' said Mrs Chisholm, stating the obvious.

The twins hung up their coats and settled in, while

Mrs Chisholm took Sylvester to 4G and Tyrone to Reception.

Tyrone became very upset and cried when Ma tried to leave. Mrs Norbury had to give him a big hug and hold him while Ma and Beyonsay left the room.

Ma was in bits on the return journey and left all the talking to Mr Carbuncle.

RRRRRRRRING!

Twelve o'clock.

Dinner time.

Channing left the classroom with a cluster of girls hanging on her arms, **chattering** like a flock of geese. Orlando was surrounded by six boys, all keen to ask him loads of questions.

They all headed for the playground, where they spotted a large group of children with Sylvester in the middle. Channing anxiously searched for a group of smaller children and soon spotted Miss Dabney holding Tyrone's hand, with half of the Reception class children hanging on to Tyrone. He seemed very happy and she began to RELAX. He did not need her at this moment.

'My name's Amelia. Do you like Little Mix? They are my favourite band.'

'I'm Jessica. What's your favourite colour? Mine is pink, of course.'

'I'm Daisy and it's my birthday next week. Would you like to come to my party?'

Avneet asked, 'What school did you go to before?'

'Where do you live?' Saffron enquired.

'I'm Cerys. Do you live in Bingham?'

All these questions at the same time! Channing was beginning to enjoy her new school until...

'Channing is an unusual name, isn't it?' Amelia queried.

'Isn't it a boy's name?' asked Megan.

THAT WAS IT! *Do I smack her now?*, Channing thought. *Or shall I make her laugh?*

She decided to make her laugh. 'My mum is really *sick*! She heard it on the news one night and thought it sounded really nice. So, that became my name. Boy or girl – I'm Channing. I don't really look like a boy, do I? Please?' Channing laughed and all the girls laughed with her.

Over the other side of the playground Alan Clampitt was telling Orlando how he went to Orlando for his holidays last year. 'How come you've got the same name?' he asked.

'My mum and dad went there on honeymoon, so they called me Orlando. I'm just glad they didn't go to Alice Springs!' He laughed. 'Imagine being called Alice! A girl's name. Ugh!'

EVERYONE LAUGHED WITH HIM.

'It's a bit like David Beckham's son Brooklyn. He's named after Brooklyn in New York,' said Alan.

'What's your name?' Orlando enquired.

'Alan Clampitt. I'm named after my dad. He's called Alan too. It gets a bit confusing sometimes.'

'Shouldn't he be called Alan 1 and you Alan 2?' Orlando asked trying to be helpful.

'Yeah, my mum does every now and then. Or sometimes she calls Dad BIG AL, and me LITTLE

AL'

'You've got an accent, you have,' said Richard Chang. 'You speak funny,' he added laughing.

Orlando laughed too.

'No I don't – *you* speak funny.' And he did an impersonation of him which made everyone laugh.

'Well, you sound like those folk that come from Birminum,' Richard persisted, giggling now.

'I do. It's a big place and it's called Birmingham not Birminum,' Orlando copied his accent again and everyone laughed.

They all went in for lunch on second sitting and, when the bell rang, they went back into class.

Here we go! Orlando was thinking. *What's this going to be like?*

CHAPTER EIGHT
Short Circuit and
Rocky VI

Orlando need not have worried. Miss Hanlon had been very busy during lunchtime. There were boxes of electrical equipment on each table.

'Please don't touch anything yet!' instructed Miss Hanlon, as several children began pulling items from the boxes on their table.

'Hector! What have I just said? Put that down and listen.'

She sounds like Ma, Orlando thought.

'Now, as you can see, you have three boxes of electrical equipment on your tables and a work sheet each. I want you to read the worksheet *first* in order to understand what you have to do. Then work as a group, or in pairs, and make sure that no one is left out.'

She scanned the faces of the children – several boys in particular – and then voiced her main concern. 'I do *not* want to see anyone playing around with the equipment. Does everyone understand? You are doing experiments and *not* playing with your XBoxes! Are there any questions?'

There were no questions. 'OK, you may begin,' she announced.

It was like a rugby scrum!

Heads down, everyone dived into the boxes, grabbing wires, bulbs, batteries and crocodile clips. There were bits falling on the floor and some children were having a **TUG-OF-WAR** over one piece of wire.

'STOP!'

Everyone froze.

'Sit.'

'Back.'

'Down.'

Miss Hanlon spoke the words with a huge gap between each and she spoke them quietly.

There were a few shuffles of chairs and one or two quiet coughs as the children sat down. All now had their eyes firmly fixed on Miss Hanlon.

SILENCE.

Orlando could hear someone breathing.

'I do not remember saying anything about behaving like lunatics at a jumble sale!' She gazed around the room at every face.

'6H, I thought we knew how to behave better than that. You've let *me* down and *yourselves*.' She stared back at the disconsolate children.

'Will someone prove that they were listening and remind us of what I asked you to do first?'

SEVERAL HANDS WENT UP.

'Yes, Megan?'

'You told us to read the worksheet first, miss.'

'Good,' Miss Hanlon said. 'At least one person heard me say it.' Then she set the trap. 'Did anyone else hear me say it?'

No one spotted it coming and everyone put up their hand.

'Oh, I see. You *did* hear me?'

'Yes, miss,' was muttered by several children. Others nodded.

'In that case, why did no one *do* it?' She spoke quietly, forcing home her advantage. 'Shall we stay in at playtime and do this work *then?* Put your hand up if you would prefer to do that.'

NO ONE MOVED.

No-one even dared to look around.

THIS WAS A PIVOTAL MOMENT AND THEY ALL KNEW IT.

'OK, let's see if we can behave like human beings this time. This is your last chance. You may begin.'

What a difference!

Orlando could not remember when he ever enjoyed a lesson so much. He was glad to find that he was on the same table as Alan Clampitt. He liked Alan. Amelia and Avneet were in the group too. They all seemed to know what to do and worked together to check each circuit.

By the end of the lesson, they had completed their worksheets and were tidying up when the bell went for playtime.

Orlando looked up to check on Channing. He could see that she was with three other girls helping Miss Hanlon to put the equipment away. So, he decided to find Sylvester in the playground and went outside with Alan, little Sydney Dench and Richard Chang.

'Do you like football?' Sydney enquired.

'Yes I like it, why?' Orlando replied, scanning the playground for Sylvester.

'We are in the school football team,' Sydney announced with a big grin on his face. 'We usually play in the playground every playtime. I'm in goal.'

Orlando looked at him incredulously. 'You're in goal? But you are so small!'

'We've got two boys in Year 3 who are taller than Sydney and he is in Year 6!' Richard pointed out, as though Sydney's height was a special achievement.

'I'm going to be over six feet tall when I grow up,' Sydney declared. 'My dad said I'll shoot up when I get older.'

'Can *you* play football, Orlando?' Alan asked.

'Well, yes, I can play.'

'Can you dribble and score goals?'

'Can you tackle?'

'Are you any good?'

'Well, I don't know. I've never been at a school long enough to join the football team!' he said with a laugh.

'Yes, but you play in the playground, don't you?' Richard asked.

'Sometimes, but not much because it ruins my shoes and Ma gets really mad with me.'

Just then a very tall lad flew past them chasing a football.

'That's Hector Vokes. He's in the football team with us,' Richard added.

'We call him Top Lip!' Alan said with a laugh.

'Top Lip. Why?' Orlando asked with a grin.

'Because his top lip is always covered in slime.

Snotty, green, slime.

Have a look when he comes past.'

Sydney added, 'He licks it with his tongue!' They all pulled a **gruesome** face, but Orlando thought it was hilarious and hooted with laughter.

They began to have a kick around with Sydney's ball and Orlando forgot about taking care of his shoes.

'We've got a football match on Wednesday,' Alan stated. 'It's the last game of the season.'

We play seven-a-side but we can only ever get six people to play!' Sydney said. 'So, we always lose!'

'Yes, we lost 6 – 0 to Hetheridge Junior School last week!'

Orlando thought this was very funny and they all *giggled* with him.

'We haven't even scored a goal yet!' Richard

pointed out and they all laughed again.

'It doesn't matter. My mum says it's the honour of representing your school that's important,' Sydney added. 'But I would like to win now and again!'

'We are playing Fordham Bridge Primary and they beat us 8 – 0 last time. Do you remember, Alan?' Richard asked. 'They've got that massive centre forward playing for them. What's his name?'

'Rocky.'

'Yeah, Rocky. He scored six of the goals.'

'Why don't you play, Orlando? That will give us seven players for the first time!' Sydney suggested. 'Sylvester could play as well. He could be sub – if he's any good.'

'Oh I don't—'

'Yes, why don't you play?' Alan encouraged. 'We could ask Mr Redding? He's just over there by the door. Come on.'

Two minutes later Mr Redding was nodding his approval.

'Do you think that Sylvester and Channing could

play too?' Orlando asked. 'They could be subs.'

'That would be a luxury!' Mr Redding grinned. 'We've never had a *full team*, let alone subs as well! OK, I will ring your mum and see what she says. You will need to come and collect permission forms from me before you go home today. Bring them back tomorrow and we will sort out kit for you all. Don't forget your boots on Wednesday.'

'I haven't got any boots,' Orlando said miserably.

'You will definitely need boots. The pitch is very slippery after all the rain we've had.'

'I've got a spare pair,' said Alan. 'I'm sure they will fit you because we are about the same size.'

'What about Sylvester and Channing though?'

'Don't worry, Orlando. I will have a look in the lost kit box for them. I'm sure there will be something in there that will fit them both,' Mr Redding responded.

THAT WAS IT.

DONE.

They were playing football for their new school on Wednesday after school. That was two days' time. And Channing and Sylvester did not know anything about it yet!

Orlando searched for Sylvester, but the bell rang and everyone lined up to go back into school. *It will have to wait for home time,* he thought.

Back in the classroom, Orlando was unable to talk to Channing because, to his **horror**, there was a test paper on each desk, and Miss Hanlon insisted on everybody being silent as they walked into the classroom.

'Now, remember children, this test will be conducted under proper test conditions and you are not allowed to talk or help each other,' she insisted.

This looks absolutely awful, Orlando thought. He put his hand up straight away. 'Please, miss, what is this?'

'It's a practice SATs paper, Orlando. We are doing them regularly now to prepare for the SATs tests next month.'

'Do we have to do them, Miss?' he continued.

'Yes, we do, Orlando. You want to do well in the SATs, don't you?'

I couldn't really care less, he thought, but said, 'I don't know what the SATs are, Miss.'

'Well this one is a science test. It will test to see what you have learned from the experiments we did before playtime. OK, everyone. You have forty minutes from now. Begin.'

ORLANDO FOUND THE NEXT FORTY MINUTES BORING AND A COMPLETE WASTE OF HIS TIME!

He could answer the questions in his head and hated having to write them down. They were easy and he had just spent a full lesson designing and testing the circuits. He could see no reason at all in going over this again.

He finished with about ten minutes to spare and spent them very profitably sketching Batman on the back of the test paper.

That put the smile back on his face!

'Time's up,' said Miss Hanlon. 'OK. Now swap with your partner and let's go through the answers.'

What? Orlando thought. *Oh no! We are going over it all **again!*** He slumped in his chair. 'Pff!' he hissed through his teeth.

Channing heard him and looked over. She knew what he was thinking and indicated with her hand for him to calm down.

Orlando looked **dejected** but swapped with Alan. Miss Hanlon called out the answers

'You've got them all correct, Orlando! Thirty-two out of thirty-two,' Alan said, impressed.

'And you have,' Orlando said swapping papers with him and **grinning.**

'Now, as we always say, we need to learn from our mistakes,' Miss Hanlon said. 'They are very important to us and tell us what we need to do to improve. So, take these papers home tonight and go through any questions you got wrong and learn from your mistakes.'

'That's my homework finished!' Alan grinned back.

'OK,' Miss Hanlon continued. 'Go and get your bags and coats and get ready for the bell.'

THE BELL RANG SECONDS LATER.

'I've got to go and see Mr Redding to get the forms,' Orlando told Alan. 'Where's his room?'

'I will come with you,' Alan replied. 'Show you the way.'

Miss Dabney appeared at the door with Tyrone. He was **smiling** and holding a painting. Channing took his hand.

'He has had a lovely day,' said Miss Dabney. 'He has painted a beautiful picture of your new house. It looks very big. I've put Teddy in his bag.'

While Channing admired this work of art, Alfred Carbuncle arrived at the cloakroom. 'Can we have all the bus children outside and on the bus in two minutes please?' He looked at Channing and asked, 'Are you all ready? I want to show you the way to the bus.'

Orlando arrived back with forms *and* Sylvester, then all four Shuffletts went out to the car park with Mr Carbuncle to get on the school bus for the very first time.

This was exciting!

There was a rule that children had to sit in the same seats for every bus journey and the Shuffletts were shown to their seats by Alfred. There was a special child seat set up for Tyrone. Channing sat next to him with Sylvester and Orlando behind.

Alfred made sure that their seatbelts were safely

fixed and reminded them where to get off. 'Don't worry, Ted, your driver knows and will call you when you get there,' he added in his Yorkshire accent.

'You sound like Postman Pat,' Tyrone giggled as Alfred checked his seat belt.

Sylvester and Orlando began to sing the theme tune. 'Postman Pat, Postman Pat, Postman Pat and his black and white cat. . .'

Alfred smiled. 'Ee by gum, you cheeky monkeys!' He joined in the song with them, laughing. 'Your mum will be waiting for you when you get off at the telephone box. See you tomorrow. Bye, bye.'

The journey was amazing!

The bus was so high that the children could see over the tops of the hedgerows into the fields beyond. They could see houses, farms and barns that they did not know existed.

'Wow! Look at that tractor!' Sylvester shouted, pointing to a huge mechanical beast that was ploughing an enormous field. He watched it for as long as he could, until it disappeared from view.

The road crossed over streams and went past woods and a church and a mansion. There were cows in several fields and sheep in many others.

'What's that?' Tyrone enquired, pointing.

'It's a scarecrow,' Channing answered.

'What is that?'

Orlando **POKED** his head through the gap between their two seats. He was pulling a face and his eyes were wide and staring.

'It's for scaring little boys! Aargh!'

'Take no notice, Tyrone,' Channing said, pushing Orlando's face back through the gap. Orlando is being silly. He's trying to scare you. Orlando, you are an idiot!'

'Just having a little bit of fun,' he countered. 'Sylvester, let's play rock, paper, scissors.'

'What does a scarecrow do?' Tyrone returned to the question.

'It is supposed to look like a man and scare the birds away so that they don't eat all the seeds,' she told him.

'It doesn't look very scary.'

'No, Orlando would look better and frighten more

birds away,' Channing laughed, turning to look at Orlando.

'Oh, ho, ho, ho, you're very funny.' Orlando **exaggerated** his laugh. Sylvester copied him, holding his belly at the same time. 'Ho, ho, ho,' they roared together.

'Shuffletts, are you ready?' Ted called out. 'We are almost at your stop.'

The bus pulled alongside the bus shelter and Tyrone shouted, 'There's Ma and Beyonsay!'

'We've got to walk all the way back up that lane now!' Orlando moaned. 'What a bellyache.'

AT LEAST IT WAS NOT RAINING.

They jumped off the bus and, after hugs and kisses all round with Ma and Beyonsay, they set off back up the lane.

'Orlando,' said Ma very calmly.

'Yes, Ma,' he replied.

'What has happened to your shoes?'

Orlando looked down. 'Pants!' he said. 'It's a long story. Can I explain when we get home, Ma? Please?'

CHAPTER NINE
Because They Can't Cook Chips!

'So, what have you all been doing today?' Ma asked, as they walked around the first bend. 'Tyrone, have you had a good day?'

'I fed the hamster,' he replied, pleased with himself.

'What hamster?' asked Channing.

'The one in our classroom. It's brown and white and I put some pellets in his dish. Then he jumped *all over them*!' he added, **shocked.**

'Did he not use a knife and fork?' said Orlando, faking astonishment.

Tyrone laughed. 'Don't be silly, Orlando. He can't use a knife and fork!'

'Why not?'

'Because they are too big for him to hold!'

Everyone laughed.

'What is that you have got in your hand?' Ma asked him, pointing to his painting.

He held it up with pride.

'Let me help,' Channing smiled, and helped him to hold up the painting.

'It's our new...' she prompted him.

'*House*!' he yelled.

'Wow!' said Ma. 'It looks fantastic. I would like to live there.'

'You *do,* silly Mummy!' he yelled louder, and they all laughed again.

'What about you, Channing? Anything special to report?'

'I made some really nice friends and one of them plays in the football team,' she replied. 'She must be really good. I'm not sure I would like to do that.'

'Oh, I bet it would be great fun,' Orlando butted in, but before he had a chance to continue, Ma spoke to Sylvester.

'Sylvester, you're not usually so quiet. Have you

had a good day?'

'It was brilliant, Ma. I've got six friends already and Marco wants me to go to his birthday party on Saturday. Can I go please, Ma?''

'That sounds exciting!' said Ma. 'I don't see why not. Where is it going to be held?'

'It's at the village hall. Marco is going to give me an invitation tomorrow.'

'OK, and what did you do in class?'

'Oh, we did some writing.' That seemed to be the end of that conversation. 'We saw a tractor on the way home,' he added with much more enthusiasm.

'*And a scarecrow!*' Tyrone **shrieked.**

'Wow, you all sound as though you have had a good time, especially after such a bad start when we missed the bus.'

'What about me, Ma?' Orlando said. 'You haven't asked me.'

'You've been playing football, Orlando, so I know what you were doing at lunchtime.'

Orlando looked thoughtfully down at his scuffed shoes and remembered the football match on Wednesday.

'There's a football match on Wednesday after school and they have asked me if I will play,' he blurted out.

'*You! Playing football!*' Channing scoffed. 'You've never played before.' She began to laugh.

The ridicule bit into him, but he pretended not to notice. 'They have only got six players and they need seven so they asked me to play.'

'But you don't even *like* football,' Channing insisted.

She was on a roll now.

'Oh yes I do!' Orlando snapped back.

'You haven't said that you are good, have you?'

Orlando was beginning to feel **anger** rise up. Ma came to the rescue. 'If you want to play football on Wednesday, Orlando, that's fine and we'll all come and watch.'

His relief turned into an enormous grin. 'Thanks, Ma.'

'I am so pleased that you are all enjoying your new school. This is definitely a *first*.'

They had arrived at the horse field, but there was

no sign of the horse.

'Where are you, horse?' shouted Tyrone.

'Where horse?' Beyonsay called. She held up both palms and looked **shocked**. 'Where horse?'

Everyone laughed.

'Clever girl!' said Ma.

THE HORSE EMERGED FROM THE BACK OF A SMALL BARN AND CAME OVER TO THEM. He put his head over the gate anticipating some food.

'We've got nothing for you this time,' Sylvester confessed. 'Can we bring him an apple tomorrow, Ma?'

'Yes,' she replied, 'but we will feed him on the way home tomorrow afternoon. We don't want to miss the bus again!'

The horse threw his head up and down several times, **snorted** loudly and ran off. 'He's agreeing with you, Ma,' Channing said with a laugh.

Ma hurried them past the "haunted house" before Orlando could start his tricks again, and soon they came to a gate. **TWO SHEEP WERE EATING GRASS UP AGAINST IT.** They moved away warily as the Shuffletts approached.

'Look! Sheep!' shouted Tyrone excitedly and ran to the gate. **THERE WERE SEVERAL MORE SHEEP IN THE FIELD.** Most of them stopped munching on the grass to look up at him.

'Aah, they are cute,' he said with a smile.

'Look, Beyonsay,' he called. 'Sheep.'

'Heep,' she said.

Tyrone laughed. 'No, "sheep,"' he corrected her.

'Heep,' she repeated. 'Heep.'

'*Sheep*!' Tyrone giggled.

'Seep,' she said and everyone laughed. Beyonsay laughed and clapped her hands.

'Good girl,' said Ma.

THE SHEEP TURNED THEIR ATTENTION BACK TO THE GRASS.

'Why do sheep eat grass?' Tyrone pondered.

'That's easy,' Orlando cut in, 'because they can't cook chips!'

Ma looked at him and burst out laughing. Channing and Sylvester joined in. Tyrone stared up at Orlando, **bewildered**, then slowly began to understand the joke and he too started laughing. Beyonsay clapped her hands enthusiastically.

Everyone laughed.

'Why do sheep eat grass?' Ma asked.

'Because they can't cook chips!' they all yelled together.

Half an hour later, they were all in the kitchen having their tea, with **NO** sign of sheep, and **NO** sign of chips.

'Right,' said Ma. 'Sylvester, you can do the washing up with Channing, while Orlando polishes his shoes.'

'Ma, did you mean it when you said I could play for the school team on Wednesday and you would all come to watch?'

'Of course I did,' she replied, 'but you've still got to clean your shoes!'

'You haven't got any football boots, Orlando,' Channing pointed out.

'That's no problem, Alan Clampitt said he would lend me some. Sylvester would you like to play as well?'

'I would love to,' he answered, 'but I don't think I am old enough.'

'Well, Mr Redding said that you can play and he

would find you some kit.'

'Really?'

'Yes. He said that they never have substitutes and it would be a luxury.'

'What's a luxury, Ma?' Sylvester asked.

'And Channing,' Orlando blurted out. 'She can play as well!'

Silence.

They all looked at him.

'They have already got a girl playing for them,' he exclaimed.

Silence.

'What's a luxury, Ma?!' Sylvester persisted.

'She won't be the *only* girl.' Orlando corrected himself. '*You* won't be the only girl. What do you say, Channing? Maybe they might win their first match if we play.'

Just when he needed some back up, Orlando received it from Ma.

'Well, if I've got to watch a football match, it would be better if you were *all* playing,' she said.

'What do you say, Channing?' Orlando persevered.

'You don't have to play if you don't want to. I just asked Mr Redding if it would be OK and he said "Yes".'

Channing folded her arms, **_thinking_** and **chewing** the inside of her lip. 'It might be fun,' she said.

'It's their last match of the season.'

'What's a luxury, Ma?' Sylvester was determined to get an answer.

'OK. I'll play!'

'What's a luxury, Ma?'

'It's something very special,' Ma replied. 'And it will be a very special football match with my three children playing!'

ORLANDO WAS MADE UP! And he went to polish his shoes with a big smile.

Later, after their chores were complete, Ma got Beyonsay ready for bed and Channing played Jenga with Tyrone.

Orlando suggested a walk to Sylvester.

He had an idea.

Once out of the house Orlando said, 'Let's go and get those eggs.' He took a carrier bag with him.

When they arrived at Arthur and Margaret's house, they **cautiously** sneaked from one bush to another until they arrived at the small pile of eggs. Orlando put them in the bag and they crept away.

They decided to go up the hill to see what was up there. The hill was very **STEEP** in places, but it was not long before they arrived at the open entrance to a caravan park built on to the side of the hill. The sign read:

The boys crept in and before them was a line of caravans. They were as **big** as houses and there were several roads leading to other parts of the park. There were caravans everywhere. Some had cars parked beside them.

'I don't think we should be in here,' Sylvester said.

'It's OK,' Orlando said calmly. 'There's no one around so it will be all right.'

They stopped when they heard voices.

Sylvester looked at Orlando.

'Over there.' Orlando pointed. 'Behind that caravan. Let's go.' He led the way, until they could see the man who had been speaking. He was sitting at a round table drinking a mug of tea.

'Would you like a biscuit as well?' a woman called out.

'No thanks,' he answered. 'I will wait until we have our bacon and eggs.'

'Let's give him some eggs now!' Orlando whispered, **giggling.**

He opened the bag and took out two eggs. 'Do you think you can throw one up in the air and make it land on his table?' he asked Sylvester. 'It will look like a bird has dropped it.'

'I'll give it a go,' he said with a titter and began to practise a few throws to gauge the distance.

'Up as high as you can and make it land on his

table,' Orlando encouraged him.

Sylvester placed the egg in his left hand, carefully positioning it up against his thumb and first two fingers. He leaned back a long way with his arm behind him, then suddenly he unleashed the egg.

UP IT WENT LIKE A ROCKET. Over thirty metres before it slowed down and began to fall back to earth.

Orlando and Sylvester hid behind a bush to watch.

Splat!

The egg landed perfectly on the table right next to the man. He recoiled sideways in fear; his arm shot up into the air, sending his tea airborne. He looked up, just in time to see the tea falling back down towards him. He tried to get up out of the way but slipped and fell onto his back and was soaked by his own tea.

THE BOYS ROARED WITH SILENT LAUGHTER.

What a result!

They watched in tight-lipped hysteria as the man stood looking at the smashed egg on his table. Then he looked to the sky, and back to the table with a **confused** expression. He seemed to be looking for the bird that had ***dropped*** the egg!

'What is the second egg for?' Sylvester whispered.

'Do it again. He won't be expecting it!'

Sylvester stood up behind the bush and took aim once more. He **unleashed** the egg and they both gawped intently as it spun through the air. This one landed on the patio right beside the man. Once again he scratched his head in confusion.

They took the remaining eggs home to Ma.

CHAPTER TEN
Just Like
Ashley Young

Ashley Young plays football for Manchester United and England. He scores goals, many of them by **BENDING** the ball right-footed around goalkeepers; usually from the left side of the pitch.

They look fantastic!

Hector Vokes, 'Top Lip' to his school friends, practices Ashley Young goals in his back garden, and in his dreams. **OVER AND OVER AGAIN.** Hector is tall and gangly and looks awkward when he runs, but he *can* make a ball bend and swerve in the air!

Just like Ashley Young.

It had been raining for most of the morning and Mr Redding almost called off the game at lunchtime but, surprisingly, the sun came out and everyone convinced him to carry on with it.

Last match of the season. **BINGHAM PRIMARY V FORDHAM BRIDGE PRIMARY.**

All nine players got changed after school and met in Mr Redding's classroom for a tactics talk. This was the first match where Bingham had a full team of seven players on the pitch. It was also the first tactics talk.

'Sydney, you will be in goal as usual,' Mr Redding began. Little Sydney Dench was the school goalie, even though he was the smallest boy in school despite being in Year 6. Sydney was **brilliant** in the small practice net in the school playground; hardly anything got past him. He would leap and dive everywhere and even *he* could reach the crossbar at 1.1m high.

But on the football pitch, in a full-size Junior goal, he looked like a **garden gnome.**

'Alan, you will be right back. Richard, you will be left back and Wyatt, you will be centre back.' He drew the positions on the whiteboard. 'Now, for the first time, we will have two players in midfield; Jessica and Orlando. That leaves Hector to play up front and,

Hector, it would be nice if you could get a goal for us today!'

Hector smiled and licked his top lip. 'I will do my best, Mr Redding. I've been practising.'

'OK. Good. Now that leaves Channing and Sylvester to come on as subs. Channing, what would be your best position?'

'I don't really know because I have never played for a team before, Mr Redding. I'm sorry.'

'I see. I think we will decide at the time where to play you. What about you, Sylvester?'

'I like to play in goal, Mr Redding,' Sylvester answered.

'Good. That means we have cover for all positions. So, we will see how the game progresses before we decide on where to use our substitutes. Any questions?'

There were none.

'In that case, let's go and enjoy ourselves.'

They ran outside and began to warm up with a few exercises and shooting skills. There was no rain now but plenty of puddles dotted the pitch.

The Fordham Bridge cars arrived and their players also began to warm up. Orlando looked over at them and spotted their centre forward, Rocky. As the lads had warned him, he was **enormous!**

The referee arrived on the pitch and Orlando stared at him in disbelief. It was *Arthur*! Artur the farter! In a proper black referee's kit! He even had proper football boots on! **ORANGE.**

Lots of parents had arrived to watch. Ma was there with Beyonsay.

'Look, it's Arthur,' said Ma.

'Artur fartur,' said Beyonsay and giggled.

Several parents began to **giggle** too. Arthur blew his whistle and called for both captains. Alan Clampitt ran to the centre circle and shook hands with the referee and then Rocky, Fordham's captain. Arthur held up a 10p coin and gave it to Alan, the home team captain. Alan **flicked** it high into the air and Rocky called out 'Heads.'

It landed in the mud and Arthur checked it. 'Tails,' he said.

Alan chose to stay at the end where they were

warming up, which meant that they would have the slight downhill advantage in the second half.

Rocky kicked off and the last game of the season was under way.

Within three minutes, most players were spattered with mud. Jessica made several **tremendous** tackles in midfield and both Alan and Wyatt stopped Rocky from opening the scoring with some desperate challenges.

But it was obvious that Fordham were the better team and, after just four minutes, Rocky scored from outside the box with a thunderous shot which sailed way over Sydney's head.

SYDNEY NEVER EVEN MOVED. HE HAD NO CHANCE.

Rocky celebrated by running to his parents at the side of the pitch to enjoy a huddle.

Orlando looked across at Sylvester and shouted, 'I haven't even touched the ball yet!'

'Bad luck, Sydney!' shouted Sydney's Mum. 'Keep your chin up.'

'How is *that* going to help?' Orlando said to

Sylvester. 'He needs *longer* arms!'

'I think the goals should be made to fit the size of the goalkeeper,' Sylvester remarked.

'Yes – that's a good idea. Sydney would only need a goal the size of a dog kennel!'

'That would be fairer,' Sylvester agreed.

Orlando soon had a chance to touch the ball. He made a tackle in midfield and sent the ball forward to Hector who dribbled past a defender, then **tripped** over the ball when it got **STUCK** in the mud. He went down quite clean and got up looking like a half-dipped chocolate biscuit.

'Well played, Orlando,' shouted Mr Redding. 'Bad luck, Hector!'

Hector smiled and licked his lip. There was more than mud on it!

Alan called to all the players, 'Don't let any of them shoot. Get a tackle in before they shoot.'

This seemed to work and, for a while, Fordham did not have a shot on target. Then, five minutes later, Rocky received the ball just inside his own half and set off at a run down the right. He cut inside and deceived

Richard with a step over. Before Wyatt could get a tackle in, Rocky hit another ferocious shot and everyone watched the ball sail over Sydney's outstretched hands into the top left corner of the net. Sydney looked devastated and his eyes welled up.

'Don't get upset, Sydney. It's *only* a game!' his mum called out.

No wonder they have never won a match! thought Orlando. *2 – 0! We are going to get hammered! I can't get anywhere near the ball. This is pants!*

The Fordham players were **jumping** up and down in celebration as if they had won the World Cup, which made the Bingham players even more devastated.

Orlando scowled and, on the touchline, Channing did the same. They looked at each other, united in defiance.

Arthur **BLEW** the whistle and Hector restarted the game, passing to Jessica.

Monty, the Fordham midfielder, ran straight at her and took the ball. He controlled it and looked to pass to Rocky again.

Not this time! thought Orlando, and he ran at the

player. Monty saw him coming and tried to turn away but Orlando managed to get a touch on the ball and **knocked** it away from him.

Orlando ran around the other side of Monty and collected the rolling ball. Looking up, he saw Top Lip making a run across the edge of the box from the centre to the left corner and sent a pass straight to him.

This was the moment Hector had been waiting for; **dreamed** about and practised over and over again. This was the situation he had watched Ashley Young do many times for Manchester United, his favourite football team.

Hector waited until the very last second. Then, he **FLICKED** the ball away behind him, back along the line of the penalty area. In a flash, *just like Ashley Young*, Hector had spun round on the spot, made one controlling touch with his left foot and lined up his Ashley Young special. He hit the ball perfectly with his right foot, creating spin and the ball looped and bent like a banana around the goalkeeper towards the back of the net.

Hector wheeled away like a gladiator, one arm high above his head in salute, his tongue on his top lip, waiting for the shouts of joy, and the high fives, and the pats, and the hugs, and the hand-shakes, and the smiles of his team-mates.

He had just scored their first goal!

'Play on!' he heard the referee call out. Arthur ran past him, waving his arms and calling **'Play on! No goal!'** Hector's smile turned to a confused frown and he turned to see the world in slow motion. The ball was stuck solid in a muddy puddle on the goal line and he watched in horror as the goalkeeper picked it up.

'That's a goal, Ref,' Hector called out and ran over to Arthur to explain why it was a goal. The rest of the Bingham players followed him.

'Come on, Ref!' someone shouted from the touchline. 'That's a goal!'

'Give it to them, Ref!' another parent called. 'They've never scored one before!' Everyone laughed.

'Go on, Ref. Be a sport,' shouted Sydney's Mum.

'Please, Arthur,' Orlando said with a sigh. 'That was a good goal.'

'Yes, it's not Hector's fault that the ball got stuck in the puddle,' Alan added.

Arthur **BLEW** his whistle to halt the game as he stood and listened to everyone, then he calmly spoke so that everyone could hear him.

'Now let me explain,' he said. 'I know it is disappointing but, it is *not* a goal because the ball did not cross the line.

'Yes, but it wou—'

'Please let me continue,' he said evenly, and looked around to make sure that everyone was listening; both on the pitch as well as on the touchline. 'You see this badge?' He held up the badge sewn onto his referee shirt and all the players strained to read it. 'This badge means that I had to pass a very hard exam to become a referee. I had to learn *all* the rules involved in football and one of the rules clearly states that the whole of the ball must cross the line before I can award a goal.'

He waited while this fact sank in.

'*None* of the ball had crossed the line from Hector's shot, so it is not a goal.'

'But if there was *not* a puddle, it would have gone

over,' Hector countered and licked his lip.

ARTHUR DID NOT HAVE TO ANSWER.
Orlando did it for him, 'But there *was* a puddle, so it was part of the pitch, Top Lip.'

'And your shot got stuck in it,' Arthur added and smiled gently at the nick-name.

'My next point is that you must *never* argue with the referee or shout at the Ref. *Ever*. It's a hard job and the referee's decision is the only one that counts. Even if we get it wrong!' He could see the disappointment on the faces of the Bingham players. 'Look,' he added. 'If this had happened to the other team, would you want me to give *them* a goal?'

NO REPLY.

'Shall we get on with the game now?'

'Yes please, Ref,' several voices answered.

'Yes,' Orlando muttered. 'Sorry, Arthur. I mean Ref. Sorry, Ref.'

As the players moved away, Arthur said in a much quieter voice, 'Orlando. Hector. That was a very good move. Why not try it again? And next time Hector; give it more wellie!' **HE WINKED.**

The boys looked at each other and smiled.

The game restarted and three minutes later Orlando set it up again. Hector was ready. This time there would be no mistakes; he was going to hit the ball higher and as hard as he could past the Fordham keeper and the puddle.

He timed his touch to perfection. Ashley Young would have been proud of that one. Then, just as the ball **bounced** off his foot, the Fordham defender came in with a bruising tackle which felled Hector and he landed with a thud on the ground just outside the penalty area.

Arthur blew for a foul and ran over to the spot where the foul had taken place. 'It's direct 'keeper,' he called to the goalie pointing to the place from where the kick should be taken.

Orlando placed the ball down and stepped back a few paces in readiness to take the free kick, hands on his hips just like the players on TV. 'Top Lip, stay close to me,' he hissed at Hector. Arthur had moved away and taken up a position in the penalty area.

Orlando whispered something behind his hand

to Top Lip.

'Come on, Orlando,' Channing shouted. 'Bend it like Beckham!' Everyone laughed. Orlando smirked.

He looked up to see that a three-man wall had been set up between him and the goal. He **scanned** around to see where the goalie was standing as well as his own teammates. Hector was standing a few metres behind him. Orlando looked at Arthur, who blew his whistle to indicate that the free kick could be taken.

He ran hard at the ball as though he was going to kick directly at the goal but, at the last split second, he laid it off one metre, and Hector, following behind him, struck it perfectly. Sweetly.

Just like Ashley Young.

The ball bent around the defenders and the goalkeeper, **STRUCK** the inside of the far post and **zipped** into the back of the net. This time he celebrated and was mugged by his teammates. They all went down in a **squirming** heap in the mud, Hector buried underneath, somewhere.

On the touchline, parents went bonkers!

Alfred Carbuncle held up his mop in salute with a

huge grin on his face. 2 – 1 at half-time. They didn't care about being a goal down.

Oranges all round from Mrs Redding.

They gathered in a small group and Mr Redding began the half-time team talk.

'Wyatt, I want you to come off for the second half because you seem to be limping at times. Alan move to the centre and Channing you can play right defence. All of you, try to stop Rocky from shooting!' He turned to look at Sylvester. 'Now, you prefer to play in goals, don't you?'

Sylvester nodded, 'Yes, Mr Redding.'

'OK. Sydney, you've played in every match so far, so I'm sure you won't mind letting Sylvester have the last twenty minutes of our season, will you?'

Sydney looked almost relieved, 'No, Mr Redding. I don't mind at all.'

'Good. That's it then. Good luck and see if you can get an equaliser!'

'Mr Redding,' said Alan, 'do you think you could get the Ref to do some keepy-uppies before the second half like he did before?'

'I will ask him,' he replied and ran off to speak to Arthur.

'You should see him, Orlando. He's amazing. He sometimes does tricks for us at half-time.'

'He used to be a footballer a long time ago,' Richard joined in. 'A proper one.'

'Yeah, he played with Trevor Francis!' Alan added.

Orlando grinned and said 'Wow!' but he had never heard of Trevor Francis.

They all turned to the centre circle where Arthur had begun his routine and for the next two minutes; everyone watched, **fascinated** and amazed by the extraordinary juggling skills of Referee Arthur Revell.

ORLANDO WAS SPEECHLESS.

'Go on, Arthur!' Channing yelled.

'Artur farter!' cried Beyonsay.

'Well done, Arthur!' Ma shouted from the touchline and everyone **CLAPPED** as he finished by balancing the ball on his head, **flicking** it up into the air and kicking it straight into the goal from the half-way line.

THE PLAYERS APPLAUDED AND RAN BACK ONTO THE PITCH. Hector got the match underway with a pass to Orlando.

The Fordham players did not seem to be alert so Orlando ran with the ball straight at their goal.

'Tackle him someone!' Monty shouted.

'Have a shot,' Arthur muttered.

Orlando heard him and let fly. The ball **sailed** harmlessly over the cross bar.

'Next time, keep your head down, over the ball. It'll go in,' Arthur murmured and ran away shouting 'Goal kick.'

The game was finely balanced. Sylvester only had two easy saves to make. A few minutes later, Orlando had the same opportunity.

He **ran** with the ball and the Fordham players seemed to back off . He ran on a few more steps and could hear Arthur's voice in his head, *'Keep your head down, over the ball.'*

He let fly with everything he had. The ball screamed into the top corner of the net and everything became a blur.

He was mobbed!

It looked as though the final score was destined to

be **2 – 2** until the last minute.

Nothing was getting past the Bingham defence and Channing was doing her part in stopping any of the Fordham players from shooting. **SHE WAS TACKLING LIKE A DEMON.**

Then Rocky began one of his mazy dribbling runs. He went past Richard and, when Alan went across to cover, Rocky nutmegged him. He was now completely through on goal with only Sylvester to beat.

You're not going to score now, thought Channing, and she raced across the penalty area and **launched** herself at him. She slid, low down and kicked as hard as she could.

Rocky **flew** in slow motion up into the air, his feet

higher than his head and they both ended in a tangled heap in the penalty area.

'Penalty, Ref!' came the cry from every Fordham player and supporter.

Arthur had no hesitation and pointed to the penalty spot (although it couldn't be seen). He had to pace the twelve steps and placed his foot at the point of the kick.

ORLANDO WATCHED AS ROCKY PUT THE BALL DOWN.

Rocky looked confident and was anticipating his hat-trick. He turned to smile at his parents. He had never missed a penalty.

Orlando watched him, fascinated.

Then, all at once, an idea came into his head and he shouted to Sylvester 'He's looking to put it to your left, Sylvie.'

Rocky overheard and frowned slightly.

Sylvester *glared* at Orlando.

'Your *left*, Sylvie.'

Sylvester looked back at him with daggers.

That will have two effects, thought Orlando. *First, that will make Sylvester very angry and will wind him up! And* secondly, Rocky won't be quite so sure now. He might even think I'm telling him to kick to Sylvie's right side.

That is exactly what Rocky was thinking. *He wants me to put it to his right. So I will put it to his left.*

Standing just outside the penalty area, behind Rocky's back, Orlando now stared back hard at Sylvester, indicating with both hands to Sylvester's *left* side of the goal. This was a gamble and Orlando knew it.

ARTHUR BLEW HIS WHISTLE. Rocky began his run-up. This was going to be his glorious triumph.

Just as Rocky's boot was going through the ball, Sylvester, full of anger for his brother, launched himself hard to his left and found that the ball was coming towards him like an express train.

He beat it away with both hands for a corner and Arthur blew the final whistle.

CHAPTER ELEVEN
Achievement
Assembly

Tyrone climbed onto the bus first, helped up by Orlando. A **LOUD** cheer went up and Orlando looked down the bus to see several children looking at him, **clapping** and cheering.

'Great goal, Orlando!' shouted Waldo Hawkes, a goofy-looking boy in Year 5.

Everyone cheered and Orlando went red! He had never experienced anything like this before. He quickly sat in his seat. He was hoping that Channing did not see. **HE FELT VERY HOT.**

Jessica Lawrence was already on the bus. She had told everyone about the match and the **fantastic** penalty save.

Channing got on next and Fatty Harris screeched, 'Here comes *Chopper* Channing! Nobody gets past her!'

Channing held her fists up like a boxer. 'Not in *one* piece!' she called back.

THERE WERE LAUGHS AND MORE LOUD CHEERS. Channing smiled and waved, then sat down in her seat in front of Orlando. Despite his efforts to cover his face, she noticed that he was blushing; something she had never seen before.

She could not resist. 'You look like a tomato!' she said.

HE PULLED HIS TONGUE OUT AT HER.

'Ketchup!' she called to him. 'Tomato face!'

The loudest cheer went up as Sylvester got on.

Hooray!

Yeah!

'What a save, Sylvester!' yelled Fatty Harris. 'You should play for England!

Sylvester looked down the bus at all the smiling faces and **grinned**. He lifted both arms up then took a bow.

'Thank you, my adoring fans.' He laughed and

squeezed past Orlando into his window seat.

'What's the matter with you? You look like you've been painted red!' he said.

Channing's face appeared through the gap in the seats. 'He's trying to be a tomato but his ears stick out too far!'

'Watch it, Channing!' Orlando snarled.

There was a whistle and a strange HISSING noise as Ted switched on the bus microphone. 'Well, everyone, I hear that we have something to celebrate today. Well done to the football team last night. What a great result!'

EVERYONE CHEERED AND CLAPPED AGAIN AS TED DROVE OFF.

Tyrone and Channing waved to Ma and Beyonsay and then settled down for the journey to school with a game of *I spy*. . .

'Are you OK?' Sylvester asked looking very concerned. His older brother was *always* in control – but not today.

'What's the matter?' Sylvester persisted. 'This is not like you.'

'I don't know,' Orlando responded. 'I've never felt so strange before. It was like... well... people have never cheered at me before. It took me by surprise. I was embarrassed.'

'You? Embarrassed?'

'People usually shout at me. They don't cheer for me. I didn't know what to say so I sat down quickly. Anyway, I'm fine now.'

And he was. The colour was disappearing from his cheeks and he said, 'Come on. Let's play *rock, paper, scissors.*'

As they arrived at school, Ted made a very ceremonious announcement over the microphone, 'Ladies and Gentlemen, the Bingham Primary School Football Team has arrived at Wembley Stadium for the final of the World Cup!' Everyone on the bus **laughed** and climbed down waving to an imaginary crowd of supporters; just like the footballers on television.

Channing pretended to be a reporter and held an imaginary microphone to Orlando's mouth saying,

'And do you think you will win the match today, tomato face?' **SHE LAUGHED AND SO DID EVERYONE AROUND.**

Orlando responded, 'Next time we have chips, I'm going to put tomato ketchup in your *socks*!'

Top Lip, Alan, Richard and little Sydney were waiting in the playground as they arrived. Everybody spoke at once! They chattered non-stop and Wyatt joined them together with a small group of well-wishers.

The bell rang and put a stop to the fun.

Miss Hanlon called the register, and then the bell rang again for Assembly.

'OK. Let's line up in silence for Achievers Assembly,' Miss Hanlon called. 'I don't want to bring anyone back here at playtime for speaking!'

No one uttered a sound and they walked in silence to sit in the school hall. Year 6 sat right at the back.

Mrs Chisholm was standing at the other end, in front of a very large screen on the wall. On a table in front of her there were all sorts of certificates and medals, and a large jar full of sweets.

Music played quietly until all classes were in and

seated. The music then faded and a bouncy, upbeat song began and a sign on the piano showed:

Celebration

Children began to sing with the song and clapped in time to the beat until that, too, had faded.

'Good morning, children.' Mrs Chisholm spoke very brightly. 'I want to congratulate you all for a week of hard work and much success. We have our awards to give out this morning and a very special announcement to make. So, let's get cracking with our Reception children.'

Amazingly, Tyrone's name was the first to be called out by Mrs Norbury, his Class Teacher. 'For a super painting of his new house, this award goes to Tyrone Shufflett, our new boy.'

Everyone **clapped** and Tyrone joined in too. Constance, sitting next to him said, 'You have to stand up and go to Mrs Norbury.'

'Why?' asked Tyrone.

'To get your certificate.'

'I haven't got a certificate,' he replied, looking rather confused, but just then Miss Dabney came to collect him and, holding his hand, she led him to Mrs Chisholm who gave him a certificate to hold up. Tyrone smiled and looked for his siblings. **THEY CLAPPED ENTHUSIASTICALLY.**

Mrs Norbury continued with her Reception achievers and, after all certificates had been awarded, each child took a sweet from the jar and sat back down. Tyrone **waved** to Sylvester as he sat back down next to Constance.

Following the Year 1, Year 2 and Year 3 awards, came Year 4, Mrs Goddard's class. She announced several awards for Maths, poetry and reading and then she said, 'Sylvester Shufflett, for settling in to his new class and making so many new friends.' She beamed and looked straight at Sylvester.

He had no idea that he was going to get a certificate so it came as a great surprise to him. He stood up and went to receive his certificate from Mrs Chisholm. He held it up with **PRIDE** and looked for Orlando, who pulled a face at him. Sylvester grinned, took his sweet and sat down.

After Mr Redding's class, it was time for the Year 6 awards.

Miss Hanlon had awarded certificates to 8 children before announcing, 'Channing Shufflett, for producing such high standards in all her work this week. What a super start to her new school!'

Channing was made up! She almost skipped up to Mrs Chisholm for her certificate.

'And finally, a family double,' Miss Hanlon continued. 'To Orlando Shufflett for his amazing

Science experiments.'

Orlando had never received a certificate before! He stood up slowly with a shocked expression on his face and went to Mrs Chisholm at the other end of the hall to receive it. **IT SEEMED A VERY LONG WALK TO HIM.**

The 6H award winners took the applause of the other children and a sweet from the jar and returned to their places. Orlando seemed in a daze and could not sit down quickly enough.

'Now, children,' Mrs Chisholm said. 'You may remember that I told you about a *special* announcement.' She paused to build the tension.

EVERYONE LISTENED INTENTLY.

You could have heard a mouse squeak!

'Well, I am going to ask Mr Redding to tell you all about it. Mr Redding, over to you.'

At the back of the Hall, Alfred Carbuncle crept in and leaned on his mop, listening. He had been waiting to hear some **good** news about the football team for the whole season. He blinked behind his thick glasses.

Mr Redding stood up and all the children **shuffled**

around to face him. 'Yesterday afternoon,' he began, 'we played our final football match of the season against Fordham Bridge Primary School and, as you know, we have not had much success in our previous games.' He looked around. 'If you remember, we lost our first game against them 8 – 0, so we were not looking forward to playing them again. In fact, if I am honest, I was dreading it!'

He laughed.

The Staff and children laughed too.

Alfred banged his mop against his mop bucket and chuckled!

'But, yesterday, for the first time, we were able to put out a full team of seven players. We even had two subs!'

AT THE BACK, ALFRED GRINNED BROADLY.

'So, let's see our nine players. Children, stand up.'

Orlando could not believe this. He had *never* stood up in Assembly before and here he was, standing up twice within five minutes! He was not quite sure whether he liked the attention. He preferred to be out of the spotlight.

SO HE REMAINED SITTING.

Mr Redding spotted him straight away. 'Come on, Orlando, stand up. You played yesterday. Don't be shy.'

This was even worse! Now **everyone** turned to look at him. He wanted to curl up into a ball and roll away but, reluctantly, he clambered to his feet. He shuffled from side to side looking uneasy.

'OK, now you children go to the front and Alan Clampitt will read the match report.'

Alan, the Captain, opened his sheet of paper and began to read. 'We won the toss and decided to kick uphill in the first half. It was very wet and we were all covered in mud. Their centre forward scored a goal very early and I thought that we needed to make some better tackles to stop them shooting.

'So, we all tried hard to stop them from having a shot at our goal.

'A few minutes later, their centre forward did some step overs and shot his second goal high into our net.

'2 – O TO FORDHAM.

'Then Hector made a great shot and we all thought he had scored our first ever goal, but the ball got stuck in the mud on the goal line. The referee told us to play on because it was not a goal. The whole of the ball has to cross the goal line for it to be a goal. We were so disappointed.

'Just then Hector was about to score but he was fouled. Orlando took the free kick and passed it to Hector who shot and this time he *did* score our first ever goal!

'2 – 1 AT HALF TIME.

'In the second half, Sydney and Wyatt were substituted by Channing and Sylvester. Orlando scored a goal and made it 2 – 2.

'Then, at the very end, Channing made a monster tackle to stop them scoring their third goal but it was a penalty.

'Their centre forward took it and Sylvester made the save of the century.

'THE FINAL SCORE WAS 2 – 2.'

Everyone in the hall **clapped** and cheered and Mrs

Chisholm presented the players with their certificates. Alfred clanged the mop bucket again and saluted like a soldier.

He was beaming!

The words of a song about trying hard and never giving up appeared on the large screen and everyone sang.

After this, the classes filed out of the hall to the bouncy beat of Kool and the Gang again.

Orlando stared at his certificates as they left the hall. This was a new experience for him and he was **surprised** and **stunned** to find that he was pleased to have them. He had not enjoyed having to stand up in Assembly, but he could not wait to get home to show his two certificates to Ma!

But his mood soon changed when they all got back into the classroom!

CHAPTER TWELVE
One For All and All For One!

O n each desk was a practice SATs paper. More SATs.

UGH!

'*Pants!*' Orlando whispered to Alan. 'More SATs practice! All you do at this school is SATs. This is the worst place ever!'

'At least it's Maths,' Alan replied. 'Better than Literacy!'

'I'd rather be drawing Batman,' Orlando said with a frown. 'But, yes... it's better than Literacy.'

They smiled and sat down. Alan looked quite keen but, for Orlando, this would be an hour of **misery**.

IT WAS!

Orlando finished after half an hour and was told to check his answers, silently, for a further ten minutes.

THIS WAS AWFUL! He pretended to go through his answers but, really, he was quite disinterested.

I've done the work, he thought. *So why do I need to check it? Isn't that the teacher's job?* He gazed out of the window. It looked quite dark – almost like night.

'OK, children. Time's up. Stop work and swap papers. We will mark them now, quickly,' said Miss Hanlon.

Soon afterwards the bell rang and a boy appeared at the door. He told Miss Hanlon that it would be a wet playtime. So everyone had to stay in their classrooms and get out the wet play games and activities.

Orlando found a nice clean sheet of paper and began to draw Batman. Now he was happy. Channing spent the time playing Connect 4 with three friends.

After about ten minutes, Amelia looked over Orlando's shoulder at his sketch. 'Wow!' That looks good,' she said quite loudly. It was more of an announcement. 'Hey, Megan, look at Orlando's drawing.'

Channing looked up smiling. She knew Orlando would not like the attention again! Several children gathered around. Orlando felt strange and quickly dropped his paper into his desk.

The bell saved him further embarrassment. End of 'wet play'.

WORSE WAS TO FOLLOW.

Miss Hanlon had given a pile of SATs Literacy papers to several children to give out. Orlando spotted what was happening. *'Pants! Pants! Pants!'* he muttered.

Channing arrived at his group with one of the piles and placed a paper on his desk. He shoved it back at her. She slid it straight back at him. Orlando gave her his best glare and shoved it back again.

'Is there anything wrong, Channing?' Miss Hanlon called.

'No, Miss,' Channing replied calmly, pulling a face that urged Orlando to stop being stupid! *Pack it in!* She mouthed at him.

HE STOPPED.

Sullenly he began to write his name on the test paper. More undiluted **boredom** followed. Orlando looked around him. Every other child seemed to be getting on with the test and some even seemed to be enjoying it!

What a palaver! he thought. *This is awful! Why doesn't something* amazing *ever happen to me?*

But he did not have long to wait before the most amazing event took place.

SOMETHING WHICH HE COULD NEVER HAVE IMAGINED ON A DAY LIKE TODAY.

Halfway through the test, a messenger arrived at the classroom door with the dreaded message:

'WET DINNER.'

There were several 'duhs' and a few 'yays'. Orlando looked straight out of the window. 'But it isn't raining, Miss!' he called out.

'Thank you for your excellent observation, Orlando, but remember to put up your hand before you speak. Please don't call out,' Miss Hanlon rebuked him.

'Sorry, Miss Hanlon,' he called out then immediately put his hand up. 'Sorry, Miss Hanlon,' he repeated, 'but if it's not raining, how can it be a wet dinner?'

'I expect it's because it is very cold and dark outside,' she answered. 'Now, let's get on with the test, shall we?'

Alan Wright whispered, 'Come with me to Mr Redding's room. He always puts a DVD on for his class. We're watching *Ice Age*.'

'That sounds good to me,' Orlando whispered back.

'Settle down now, boys.' Miss Hanlon **GLARED** at them.

Outside it began to brighten, but then it started to rain.

Remarkably, the rain turned to sleet and then to snow. Then to great big snowflakes.

There was a lot of nudging and pointing until, eventually, everyone was staring at the windows. The snow fell like silent confetti at a wedding and someone shouted, 'It's sticking!'

Several children, furthest from the window, stood up to see for themselves and two boys charged over to get a better view. 'Sit back down, children, and get on with your test. You have five minutes left,' said Miss Hanlon.

'Oh, but, Miss—'

'No "buts", Hector. Now do as you are told. We've got to get this test marked before lunch.' Miss Hanlon reprimanded him.

FINALLY...

Eventually...
Mercifully...

THE BELL RANG FOR LUNCH.

'Now listen carefully, my little snowflakes,' Miss Hanlon began. 'Remember, no one is allowed outside and you are on second sitting, so you will go for lunch at 12:30. Wet play monitors can get out the games and activities and you can begin.' She left, heading for the peace and quiet of the staff room.

Children began to open boxes of games and the **noise** level ramped up a few decibels. Alan Wright checked that Miss Hanlon was out of sight, looked at Orlando and said, 'Let's go.' Wyatt and Top Lip joined them and they headed for Mr Redding's room.

Sylvester appeared in the corridor with Marco Sennellini coming towards them. They made **high fives** all round and Sylvester asked, 'Where are you lot going?'

'Mr Redding's room to watch *Ice Age*. Where are *you* going?'

'We're bored so we are just having a walk around. I really want to go outside and throw some snowballs.'

'That's a great idea!' Top Lip shrieked. 'Let's do it!'

ORLANDO ALREADY HAD HIS HAND ON THE DOOR HANDLE.

'Roll up! Roll up! Walk this way, boys – to the snowball fairground. There's only one rule though...'

'What's that?' Wyatt asked.

'Sylvester is on *my* side! After all, he *is* my brother.' Orlando **smirked** at Sylvester who GRINNED back like a Cheshire cat. Between them, they were a formidable throwing team.

'Agreed!' they all shouted and ran out into the cold.

They had no idea how cold it would be and they

all gasped as they breathed in the freezing cold air. They stared at the snow. The playground looked like a huge cake covered in smooth white icing.

Sylvester bent down to scoop up snow for his first snowball. Hector seized his chance like a true centre forward and kicked snow all over him. Sylvester roared his disapproval and squeezed the snow into a ball. He knew exactly who would receive this little beauty.

Scooping up handfuls of snow, the boys all threw their first snowball at the nearest boy to them. Top Lip caught the little beauty from Sylvester right in the middle of his face. **HE SCREAMED!** Everyone laughed and Top Lip wiped the cold wet snow from his face together with a long, stringy sliver of green slime.

This made Orlando laugh even more.

With a roar, Top Lip gave chase to Sylvester and hurled a large snowball which missed him. Orlando followed up to protect his brother and launched his snowball at Hector. He missed too but Alan, following them both, heaved a beauty which landed on the back of Orlando's head and sprinkled down his neck!

Orlando squealed.

Everyone laughed again and Orlando and Sylvester gathered up more snow and began to chase Alan. This turned out to be a big mistake!

Alan ran straight to Wyatt and Marco who had been making several snowballs and all three of them launched a volley of snowballs at the brothers.

In vain, Orlando and Sylvester tried to make snowballs of their own to return fire, but they were getting hit too often now. They were under attack from a well-prepared enemy and they **collapsed** in a heap, rolling in the snow laughing and giggling, and whisking huge plumes of snow up into the air.

EVERYONE DIVED ON TOP. It was like a game of rugby. They were all trying to stuff snow down each others shirts.

'Let's roll a snowman,' Orlando suggested.

So they did. In fact they rolled three. Orlando and Alan worked together and so did Hector and Wyatt.

Marco and Sylvester did their best, but their snowball was much smaller than the older boys' efforts. Hector and Wyatt's snowball was the biggest.

They stopped rolling when it got too **HEAVY** to roll anymore; just outside Mrs Chisholm's office window! Fortunately, they did not notice and fortunately, Mrs Chisholm was out.

'I know,' suggested Orlando. 'Let's put our snowball on top of yours, then we can put the little one on the top.'

'Yeah, that should look good,' said Hector, sniffing. He had a huge, frozen, green ball on his top lip.

Orlando looked at it and was hysterical. He had never seen anything like it before. Top Lip carefully removed it and threw it away. The four oldest boys **struggled** hard to lift the second snowball into place, and then helped Marco and Sylvester put theirs on the top with satisfied pride.

Wyatt and Top Lip filled in the ridge between the two big snowballs so that it looked like one body.

'We'd better go,' said Alan. 'I think we might be late.'

They did not know how close they had come to being seen for, as they left the huge snowman to go back inside, Mrs Chisholm arrived back in her office.

She was too busy to notice the white blob sitting just on the other side of her window.

Without knowing it, they had just had a very close escape. But, as they **stamped** off the snow from their shoes, they realised that they were all very wet and had cold, numb fingers.

They CREPT inside and Alan said, 'We are in trouble now. We can't go in for lunch like this. Someone will spot that we are wet and cold.'

'Do not worry, my Captain,' Orlando said. 'Orlando to the rescue!'

'What do you mean?' Alan queried.

'Quick. Let's change into our PE kit, warm our hands under the warm water and pretend we've got PE after lunch!'

'Brilliant!'

'You're a genius!' said Top Lip.

'Leave our wet clothes on the radiator to dry and we can put them back on before Miss Hanlon gets back,' Orlando added.

Five minutes later, they were queuing for lunch in the dining room and nobody even questioned them in their PE kit.

'We've got away with it, lads!' said Orlando triumphantly when they were sitting down eating. 'High fives all round.' They all looked very pleased with their daring escapade.

Getting caught was the risk you took when you did something **DARING.** The six of them had been *daring*. Very daring and had got away with it. They had not done anything wrong (or naughty) – only *daring*.

And fun!

They were *so* pleased with their success.

Orlando hated being caught. **THERE WAS NO FUN IN THAT!** They had got away with it. Now *that* was something *special*. Something to be enjoyed.

He did not know it yet, but his luck was not going to hold out for much longer. 'OK,' he said, as they changed back into their school uniforms which were still steaming on the radiators. 'Let's do this again at playtime!'

'That's a great idea!' the others cried.

'We are like the Three Musketeers,' Alan said.

'What do you mean?' Wyatt asked. 'There are *six* of us!'

'Well, they were all friends and very daring and they used to say *'One for all, and all for one!'* Alan explained.

'I don't know what that means, but you can count me in,' Top Lip chirped.

'One for all, and all for one!' they chanted together and they held up their water bottles in salute.

After lunch, the dining room and kitchen staff cleaned up and had their own lunch together. It's usually a raucous affair with the ladies having a good laugh about anything: TV, *Eastenders*, the children, the daft things they say or what they will be doing that night or at the weekend.

Today they were a bit worried about getting home in the snow.

Mrs Culpepper was especially worried. She was **extremely** overweight and could not walk very well in normal conditions. The children called her 'The fat dinner lady'. They said once around her was the same as three times around the town! **CHILDREN CAN BE SO CRUEL.**

'I don't know how I'm going to get home,' she wailed to the others. 'It's so dangerous walking in the snow.

'Just go slowly, Ursula,' said Mrs Bagette, the Cook. 'Slow and steady.'

'You can hold my arm,' said Martha.

'And mine,' said Daisy. 'I can go your way. I've got to go to Clampitts to get some food for tea tonight.'

They finished eating and tidied away just in time to get their coats on as the bell rang for playtime.

'Those poor kids have been stuck in all day,' said Martha.

'Yes, and they are going to be stuck in again now. It's been snowing for the past two hours so there is no way they will be let out,' Ursula added.

Little did she know!

At that very moment, six boys were creeping out into the playground to finish a snowman and to have a second snowball fight!

'See you tomorrow, if it stops snowing,' Martha shouted to everyone.

A chorus of 'see you' followed from everyone in the kitchen.

The three ladies stepped out into the cold and into 75mm of freezing wet snow and were instantly struck by three snowballs, which landed on their very ample backsides!

'Ooa!'

'Oops!'

'Oh my giddy aunt!'

The three ladies shrieked as they clung on to each other, **TERRIFIED**. Somewhere behind them they could hear boys **laughing.**

They slipped but did not fall. They **staggered** and **struggled** to keep themselves upright, gripping each other tightly.

Suddenly, another bombardment of snowballs pelted them from behind. They could hear lots of laughter but were too frightened to turn around in case they slipped and fell over.

Ursula Culpepper knew that if she fell down, she would not be able to get back up in this slippery snow.

SYLVESTER WAS HAVING A BALL. These three ladies were easy targets and he had not missed once.

'Three, two, one, fire!' Orlando called and another barrage of snowballs burst on the ladies, covering them with snow.

'This is brilliant!' shrieked Top Lip.

'Quick!' shouted Daisy. 'Let's get back inside before we all get killed!'

They turned to head back to the kitchen door and

snowballs burst all over them again. One snowball landed on Martha's neck and **dribbled** down her back. It was cold and wet and she yelped.

The ladies **burst** through the kitchen door in a hail of snowballs and snapped it shut. Mrs Culpepper was in tears. **OUTSIDE EVERYTHING WENT QUIET AND STILL.**

The six boys stood very still now. In fact, they looked like statues, frozen in place. Orlando released his last remaining snowball and it dropped softly into the snow. They were all looking at one window. **Horrified.** Looking back at them was Mrs Chisholm.

Five minutes later, all six boys were standing in her office looking very uncomfortable.

'As well as writing a letter of apology to each of the three lunchtime supervisors you attacked, you will forfeit every playtime for a week and spend the time here in my office tidying up and doing useful jobs.'

Mrs Chisholm was laying it on thick. She **EYEBALLED** each of the boys in turn. 'Do I make myself clear?'

They each managed to mumble, 'Yes, Mrs Chisholm.'

'Every lunchtime for the week will be spent helping the staff in the kitchen, scraping plates, rinsing dishes, wiping tables and anything else that needs doing. Do I make myself clear?' she asked again.

'Yes, Mrs Chisholm.'

'And finally, you will apologise to your parents for letting them down so badly. Do I make myself clear?'

'Yes, Mrs Chisholm.'

'Good. All this will take place after the Easter Holidays which begin tomorrow. You will be going home early today because of the snow and school will be closed tomorrow for the same reason. We don't want you coming into school attacking adults again, do we?'

'No, Mrs Chisholm.'

CHAPTER THIRTEEN
No Business Like
Snow Business!

The snow was still there the following morning.
'Yesss!' Orlando hissed, looking through his bedroom window. 'It's even deeper!' he muttered to himself, **grinning.**

He charged to his brothers' room and threw open the curtains.

'Wake up you two!'

'It's even deeper!' he yelled at the top of his voice. 'Look!' he insisted.

Sylvester and Tyrone sat up sleepily. 'Come and look, you dozy scarecrows,' Orlando called to them. 'It's still here. And it's deeper!'

The boys dragged themselves to the window and

stared out.

'Wow!' said Tyrone.

'Yeah, wow!' Orlando copied.

The snow was ankle deep in places. **Perfect.**

School was closed because of it. **Perfect.**

This should have been the *last* day of school before the Easter holidays, but it was now the *first* day of the holidays. **Perfect.**

No SATs tests. Two weeks of freedom. **Perfect!**

Orlando was content.

Tyrone stared in disbelief – he had never seen snow like this before. **EVER!**

There was snow as far as he could see and the trees and bushes looked black.

It was a strange sight.

His brothers were grinning. He joined in. They looked at each other, made high fives all round, then raced down for breakfast.

Ma was helping Beyonsay with her scrambled egg and Channing was writing in her big notebook, taking the occasional mouthful of cereal. She looked up briefly as the boys rushed into the kitchen.

'Orly! Sivee! Ty-Ty!' gurgled Beyonsay, clapping her hands. Scrambled egg flew over Ma's face.

THE BOYS LAUGHED RAUCOUSLY.

Ma wiped the egg from her nose and eyebrow. 'Thank you, Beyonsay, but I think I'll have cereal today!'

Beyonsay giggled and clapped again. Ma flinched as more **EGG** flew through the air.

'What are you doing, Channing?' Orlando scoffed. You're not practising for those barmy SATs tests, are you?'

'No,' she replied thoughtfully. She seemed preoccupied and, for once, she did not bite back. 'I'm trying to write a poem about that scarecrow we saw the other day.'

'But it's been snowing all night! There's snow *everywhere*!'

'They just seem to stand and watch everything,' Channing continued wistfully.

'Yes, come on. Let's go and throw snowballs,' Sylvester said, trying to encourage her.

'I wonder what they would think if they were alive,' she persisted, lost in thought.

'I wish we had a sledge,' Orlando said with a miserable groan. 'We could go sledging on the hill.

'That would be amazing!' Sylvester responded.

CHANNING MADE UP HER MIND. 'I'm going to call it "A Scarecrow, watching".'

'That sounds a lovely title for a poem, Channing,' Ma said encouragingly.

'If Dad was here, he would get us a sledge,' Orlando remarked dejectedly.

'Why don't you ask Arthur if he has a sledge that you can borrow?' Ma suggested, changing the mood. She did not want them moping about the house getting bored.

They would only end up arguing or fighting!

'That's a good idea!' Sylvester said enthusiastically. 'Come on, let's go and ask him.'

'Are you going to come with us, Channing?' Orlando asked.

'Might. What about you, Ma? Fancy going sledging?' she asked in a mocking tone.

'I would *love* to see that!' Orlando hooted.

Ma was quick to respond. 'Let me tell you, I used to go sledging and ice skating before I met your dad. I was very good too!'

Everyone laughed at the thought, except for Orlando.

'Oh, I wish Dad could be here to join in,' Orlando said. **HE SEEMED QUITE SAD.**

'He will be here soon enough,' Ma said, realising she had made a mistake mentioning Dad. She ushered them out of the kitchen. 'Now go and see if Arthur has a sledge.'

They grabbed their coats, gloves and wellies and went outside into ankle deep snow. Ma stepped out into snow, still wearing her slippers. She grabbed Tyrone and wrapped a scarf around his neck.

'That will keep you extra warm,' she said, and gave him a hug, then a kiss on his cheek. This would be his first walk without her. 'Stay by your brothers and do as they tell you, OK?'

He nodded.

Channing joined her, wearing a coat, and a smile.

'Hey, Ma,' she said. 'This will be Tyrone's first snow. Wasn't he a baby the last time it snowed?'

'That's right,' said Ma, putting her hands into her pockets to protect them from the wind. 'Have a good time, boys.'

They boys ran out **giggling** and *laughing,* kicking the snow up into the air. Tyrone was overjoyed.

The snow was dry and powdery and kicked up like talcum powder, covering them, sticking to their faces then melting, cold and wet!

They laughed and shrieked with excitement.

Orlando scooped up a handful of snow and threw it at Sylvester.

Sylvester saw it coming and **DUCKED**. The snowball flew past him exploding with a quiet *'thud'* on the wall of the house. It was an appealing sound that made them all laugh. The snow stuck like a white star.

Sylvester copied. **Thud!**

Laughing, they all began to pepper the wall with snowballs.

Thud!

Thud!

Thud!

Tyrone scooped snow and made a kind of snowball, which fell apart when he tried to throw it.

Most of the snow landed on his head! He giggled. 'I can see my breath!' shouted Sylvester. 'Look! Breathe out.'

They all breathed out together and watched the silver 'smoke' as their hot breaths met the cold air. Sylvester took an **ENORMOUS** deep breath and blew out a huge, billowing stream of silver steam. Tyrone giggled and copied.

Orlando turned and ran, **JUMPING** into a sideways slide on both feet; his arms open wide like a tightrope walker. The other two copied but Tyrone fell over into the snow.

Laughing, his brothers took one hand each and hauled him to his feet, then set off up the lane to Arthur and Margaret's house. Tyrone was in the middle, holding hands with his elder brothers. For once, his teddy had been left behind. Orlando and Sylvester skidded and slid in the deep snow. Tyrone **squealed** and **giggled** as he copied them. They pulled him faster and faster until his legs could no longer keep up, so he simply stood upright, **SKIDDING**, as they pulled him along. Tyrone shrieked with delight.

This was amazing fun!

'You're skiing!' yelled Orlando.

'Yeah, I'm skiing!' Tyrone shouted. 'What's skiing?'

A huge tractor swung noisily down the hill towards them just as they arrived at Oak Cottage. It filled the whole width of the lane and its tyres were taller than Orlando! The boys leapt to the safety of Arthur's drive.

'Wow, look at that!' Orlando shouted as the tractor thundered past them. They stood, staring and panting breathlessly. The man sat high up in the cab and waved to the boys. **THEY WAVED BACK.**

As soon as it had gone past, the boys rushed out on to the lane to look at the tyre tracks in the snow. The tyres had squashed the snow flat and left two deep ruts with patterns. Orlando and Sylvester could not resist walking in the ruts like tightrope walkers, arms out to the side.

Tyrone squatted down in the tracks to examine the pattern left by the tyre treads. He was **FASCINATED** but when he looked up, his brothers had disappeared into Arthur's drive.

'Wait for me!' he shouted, running to catch them up, slipping and sliding as he did so.

Artur the farter was in his workshop.

'Hello, Artur,' they chirped together.

'Hello, boys. What brings you around here? I see you're not at school today.'

'No, it's closed because of the snow,' Orlando responded.

'We want to go sledging,' Sylvester announced.

'Sledging?' Arthur said. 'That sounds like a lot of fun!'

'Well, it would be if we had a sledge. We were hoping you might have one we could borrow, Arthur,' Orlando said hopefully.

Arthur looked back at them somewhat dejectedly. 'No, I'm sorry, I don't have one.'

He watched the boys' faces *drop* with

disappointment.

'But I could make you one right now if you are not in a hurry.' Arthur looked at the boys questioningly. 'I don't think the snow will disappear in the next twenty minutes.'

'You could make one right now,' Orlando said incredulously. 'Actually *make* it?'

'Yes.'

'Right now?'

'Take me about twenty minutes,' Arthur responded with a smile. 'I'll make one for each of you if you'd like!'

The boys looked at each other and grinned.

'Wow!'

'Yes, please!'

'OK, now you three sit over there and don't move. Some of this machinery is very dangerous. And noisy, so you might want to cover your ears.'

THE BOYS PULLED THEIR HOODS OVER THEIR EARS.

Arthur smiled and selected a large piece of wood and began marking it using his tape measure. Within three minutes, he had cut it into smaller pieces on one of his machines.

'You two boys played really well in the match on Wednesday,' he said to the two older boys as he worked. 'That was a super goal Orlando, and a great penalty save, Sylvester.'

'Thank you,' they both muttered, captivated by Arthur's ability at making sledges.

Arthur took a much wider, THICKER piece of wood and cut that too. He curved the ends on another machine and then, finally, he used a nail gun to fix every piece in place.

HE HAD MADE THREE SLEDGES IN FRONT OF THEIR EYES.

'I thought they were going to win the game when Channing gave away the penalty,' he added.

'So did I,' said Orlando. 'It was the only thing she could do because Rocky was completely through on goal.'

'True. Now, we need to make the runners smooth so they glide over the snow.'

He switched on a machine and a wheel began to

spin. He held each runner against it and smoothed the wood.

He fixed one piece of wood to each side of the sledges with a metal bolt as a pivot so that they could move.

'You hold on to those with your hands. They are the controls,' Arthur announced.

Next he drilled two small holes at the front of each sledge.

'What are those for, Arthur?' asked Orlando.

'To tie your string through so you can pull the sledge up the hill.' He took down a ball of bright blue nylon rope and tied the pull cords in place. 'Done!' he announced. 'Be careful though, they are heavier than plastic sledges but they should be much stronger. You will just have to eat more beans for energy!'

'Wow! Arthur, they are amazing. Thank you,' said Orlando.

'Thank you, Arthur. Thank you very much. We can go and have some fun now,' said Sylvester.

'Thank you, Artur,' squealed Tyrone.

'Just promise me you will not use them on the lane.

You don't want a tractor to come along and squash you like a steam roller!'

'Promise!' they said together.

The boys ran out of the work shed and down Arthur's drive to the lane where the two older boys immediately **dropped** their new sledges into the snow and leapt on them, on their bellies, to glide SMOOTHLY in the deep snow between the tractor tracks. Tyrone copied and was soon on his way down the hill too. Snow **flew** up into their faces, up their noses and into their mouths. They **SHRIEKED** with the coldness and the excitement of it. It was now quite difficult to see.

They cheered and laughed until, suddenly, the tractor came back the other way, going fast – too fast for the boys to get out of the way!

The driver looked alarmed and slammed on his brakes and the tractor came to a rapid halt.

But the boys did not.

The boys continued sliding – *straight under the tractor*. Orlando first, rapidly followed by Sylvester. Orlando could see that it was like being in a tunnel and let out a loud 'Yippee!'

SYLVESTER SCREAMED. THIS WAS FRIGHTENING.

Orlando emerged from the back of the tractor and immediately rolled off his sled. It was the only way he could get it to stop. He was almost completely buried in snow and was now laughing.

Sylvester did *not* roll off his sled and **ploughed** into Orlando's legs. His sled came to a sudden halt and Orlando shrieked in pain.

'Aargh! Sylvie! Watch it. That hurt.'

Tyrone gently bumped into Sylvester's sled and he began to laugh.

Orlando rubbed his PAINFUL leg and looked up at the driver in the tractor cab. He was leaning back looking through the rear window and laughing.

'He's laughing at us, Sylvie, look.' He pointed up at the cab.

Sylvester's ambition was to become a cricketer. More than anything else, he wanted to be England Captain, like Alastair Cooke.

HE WAS NOW ANGRY. TWICE ANGRY.

He did not *ever* like to be called Sylvie, and he did *not* like farmers laughing at him. Especially when they have just driven over him!

SYLVIE WAS ANGRY.

He stood up, made a snowball and threw it as hard as he could. Cricketers have to be good at throwing and Sylvester was good. He was aiming straight at the farmer's face but the snowball **exploded** on the glass window. The farmer laughed even more.

Sylvie threw another snowball and Orlando joined in. They **SHOWERED** the window with snowballs until they could hardly see the farmer inside.

The farmer opened his door and leaned out, laughing loudly. 'Is that the best you can do?' he goaded.

Sylvester's next snowball caught the farmer right in the face and he almost fell out of the cab, spluttering.

Orlando yelled with delight. 'Yeah!'

'You asked for it,' the man said, jumping down into the snow. He was a huge, stocky man with a big belly. He immediately rolled a snowball and threw it at Sylvester. It sailed past HARMLESSLY and the boys laughed.

'Is that the best you can do?' Orlando shouted, mimicking the farmer. Sylvester let fly his next snowball which landed with a thud on the farmer's big belly.

The boys laughed and made another snowball each.

Farmer Big Belly bent down to gather his next snowball and the boys **PELTED** him. Snowballs **exploded** on his head, his back and his ample bottom. The farmer ROARED like a lion and returned snowballs as fast as he could, but he was much slower than the two boys. Nevertheless, he was enjoying this and he began to laugh, then Arthur appeared with Floss.

Arthur summed up the situation in a **flash** and joined Farmer Big Belly in the snowball fight of the year.

'Morning, Cecil. You've got your hands full here!' Arthur called out. 'Looks like you need some help,' he said with a laugh.

'No. I've got 'em cornered. They're ready to give up any minute now!' Cecil replied and winked at Arthur. Snowballs RAINED down and Floss raced around from one to another, leaping up and down and barking **WILDLY.** Tyrone seemed to get more snow on himself than anyone else but he was having fun.

'Help!'

Floss was having a **WONDERFUL** time and she leapt high trying to catch snowballs. Now and then, she managed to catch one in her teeth which made her snort and sneeze, but did not stop her.

'Help!'

The fight moved further down Arthur's drive as the two men searched for more fresh snow to throw.

'He-e-e-elp!'

Behind the boys, a red van pulled up and Postman Pam climbed out. She immediately joined in and began to pelt the boys from behind. The boys were now forced to throw snowballs on two sides.

'He-e-e-e-elp!'

'Morning, Pam,' shouted Arthur.

'Morning, Arthur. Morning, Cecil,' she called back. 'Looks like I'm just in time to stop you two from getting a beating!'

'We don't need no 'elp, Pam. We've got these three squirrels trapped now. They ain't going nowhere!' replied Cecil, and they all roared with laughter.

'He-e-e-e-e-elp!'

'HE-E-E-E-E-ELP!'

'He-e-e-e-e-elp!'

Everyone stopped.

LISTENING.

Straining to hear.

'He-e-e-e-e-elp!'

'Did you hear that?' Arthur asked.

Everyone nodded, listening.

'I heard somebody shouting for help,' said Orlando.

'He-e-e-e-elp!'

'Someone *is* calling for help somewhere,' Pam agreed.

'Sounds like it's coming from up there on the bank,' said Cecil, pointing to the hill.

The hill!

The hill!

The hill was everyone's nightmare in **snOW** or **Ɪꞔꞓ** or **FROST**. It was impossible for any vehicle except a tractor to get up or down the hill in **snOW** or **Ɪꞔꞓ** or **FROST.** It was so steep with a dangerous precipice on one side.

'Someone is stuck on the hill!'

The grown-ups looked very concerned.

CHAPTER FOURTEEN
Over and Out

The voice was clear – faint, but clear. Sound carries further in the countryside than in the town.

'He-e-e-elp!'

'Somebody's in trouble all right,' Cecil muttered with a grim expression.

'Well, I most definitely won't be able to get up the bank in my van,' said Pam the Postie. 'I'm only going as far as the caravan park anyway. I'll wait there and, if it is serious, you will have to get a message to me. I can ring the emergency services on Jeffrey's landline because you won't get a signal on your mobile on the bank.'

'No, don't you worry, Pam. I'll get this sorted,' said Farmer Big Belly, looking serious for the first time that morning. 'I'll give 'em a toot on the horn to let 'em know we're on our way.'

He swung **EXPERTLY** into the cab of the tractor and sounded the horn several times.

TOOT!

TOOT!

TOOT!

TOOT!

'Help!'

He tooted again; longer this time.

TO-O-O-O-OT!

Then he leaned out of the cab, standing on the footplate, looking up the hill and called out, 'Can you hear me?'

There was a long pause.

'Yes!' came a faint reply.

'OK, I'm on my way.' Farmer Cecil Big Belly paused and then added, 'Are you hurt?'

Another long pause.

'No, but my daddy...' The voice drifted away. '...in the snow.'

Cecil, Arthur and Pam exchanged **anxious** glances.

Orlando understood the worry on their faces and said, 'Please can I come with you to help?'

'No, I'm sorry, son,' replied Farmer Cecil. 'You would only be in the way.'

'But there are at least two people up there. I could help one of them while you help the other.' Orlando's mind was **TICKING** over with the thought of a rescue mission on a tractor.'

'He has a point, Cecil,' said Pam.

'Yes, but it could be dangerous, Pam. You know how bad that hill can be.'

'Help!'

'I could bring a message down to Pam so she could ring 999,' Orlando said, looking earnestly at the farmer.

'He's got another good point, Cecil,' Arthur joined in.

'Yes, but how would he get back down safely?' Cecil responded. 'How old are you, boy?'

'I'm ten.'

'I'm sorry but it's out of the quest—' Cecil was interrupted.

'He-e-e-elp!'

They all **LOOKED** across the field and up the wooded hillside searching for the voice.

'I could use my sledge,' Orlando suggested holding it up for examination. 'It's got two brakes. I could come back down to Pam on my sledge. Please let me help.'

'Hurry! He-e-e-elp!'

'You need to make a decision, Cecil,' Pam prompted.

Cecil stood staring at Orlando, then at the sledge,

then back at Orlando.

'Let's go!' he said and he hoisted Orlando into the tractor cab. 'Arthur, can you look after the two young lads till we get back?' Orlando could not hide his pleasure and he **grinned** down at Sylvester.

'Of course I can. You get going and help those people,' Arthur replied, pulling Sylvester and Tyrone close to him. 'And you, Orlando, take care and do as you're told. OK?'

ORLANDO NODDED.

Cecil swung up into the tractor. He checked that Orlando was safely belted into his seat and started the engine. 'So, they call you Orlando, do they? I've been to Orlando many times. It's lovely there. Nice and warm.'

He waved and set off towards the hill. The tractor went very quickly, as though there was no snow at all.

Orlando was not sure if this was a good idea after all. He did not know if he was **scared** or excited, but he felt very strange. This was scary *and* exciting at the same time!

The tractor roared up the long hill around the

bends, until it came to the steeper part near Arley Fields Caravan Park. Orlando thought that Cecil would slow down but, instead, he went faster.

The hill became very

                      steep

                            and

                                he

                                    could

                                        see

                                          a

                                      sharp

                                      bend

                                    300

                                  metres

                                  ahead.

'They'll probably be around the bend and up the next stretch. That's the steepest part of the bank,' Cecil reflected. 'That's where most folks get into trouble in the snow.'

They were approaching the right hand-bend. This was much too fast for Orlando's comfort, but Cecil seemed to know what he was doing. **HE EVEN BEGAN TO HUM TO HIMSELF.**

Orlando found himself gripping the sledge so tightly that his fingers were hurting. He relaxed them and looked to his right and immediately wished that he had not.

The bank ran away steeply, almost like a cliff! Orlando froze, staring at the precipice with complete dread. He imagined the tractor sliding off the road and rolling over and over down the bank. There were bushes and trees growing over the bank. Orlando wondered if they would be strong enough to stop the tractor from rolling to the very bottom.

'There they are!' shouted Cecil with satisfaction, pointing at a car near the top. The hill was very **STEEP** and the car was stranded at an angle across the lane. As they got closer, it became clear that the back left-hand wheel was not actually on the road, but in a deep snow-filled rut and resting against the low Hawthorn hedge. The car was **DANGEROUSLY** close to the edge and looked ready to topple over it. Standing by the side, and holding on to a door handle was a young girl, who looked about eight.

'Oh my giddy aunt!' Cecil said. 'What have we here?'

ORLANDO WAS TERRIFIED AND SAT, FROZEN, STARING.

Cecil pulled up very close to the car. 'Orlando, you wait here until I call you. OK?'

Orlando did not need to be told twice! **HE WAS PETRIFIED.**

Cecil jumped down and carefully made his way to the girl. He did not want to alarm her so he smiled and said, 'Hello, my name's Cecil. What's your name?'

'Carla,' she answered. 'My daddy's down there.' She pointed to the sheer drop.

Cecil's heart sank. This was not going to be a simple towing job. He smiled again to hide his fears. 'Has he gone for a walk then?' he asked.

'No, he fell backwards over the hedge. He's in the snow. He can't move.'

Cecil knew he had to look, but was **DREADING**

what he would see.

'OK. Now, can you see Orlando up there in the lovely warm tractor?'

'Yes,' said Carla, nodding.

'Well I'm going to pick you up and take you to him. Is that OK?'

CARLA BEGAN TO CRY. 'My daddy can't move. He's in the snow. I want my daddy.'

'Don't you worry, little lady. I'll get your daddy and then we can all go and have a nice cup of tea. How does that sound?'

'I don't like tea,' she said, with tears streaming down her face.

'Oh dear! What do you like instead? Whisky?'

'No silly! Hot chocolate,' Carla managed to smile through her tears and giggled.

'Right then. Come on, let's get you into the tractor. And we can all have a hot chocolate when we get down the hill. That sounds like a great idea to me.'

Cecil picked Carla up and carefully made his way to the tractor, trying not to slip. He gently lifted her into the cab alongside Orlando.

It was nice and warm.

'You two wait there for me while I get your dad.' Cecil smiled.

He closed the door and cautiously edged towards the hedge. Suddenly he lost his footing and both feet flew into the air.

CECIL LANDED ON HIS BOTTOM IN THE SNOW! He looked up and the two children were laughing at him.

He shook his fist with **pretend** anger and cautiously stood up. He was now very fearful of what he would find on the slope. Gingerly he leaned out over the hedge and grabbed hold of a large branch for support. He felt the thorns dig into his fingers and **grimaced** with the pain. He could see nothing but the snowy, steep slope, trees and thorn bushes.

'Hello,' he called. 'Hello. Can you hear me?'

'I'm here,' a voice replied.

'I can't see you,' Cecil responded.

'I'm directly below the car. I fell over backwards trying to clear the snow from the tyre. I'm covered in snow, stuck in the thorn bush, and I can't get out.'

Cecil searched the snow, following a skid track down to the bush. About ten metres down, he could see a pair of legs.

The man was upside down!

'I see you!' he called. 'Are you all right? Are you injured?'

'I'm freezing cold but I don't think I've broken any bones. I'm just trapped by some thorns.'

Cecil calmly assessed the situation. 'I need to get some tools to cut you out and a rope to get down to you. Give me a few minutes.'

'I'm not going dancing just yet,' the man said with a laugh.

Warily, Cecil **scrambled** back to the tractor. Quickly he collected a pair of cutters and a snow spade from a container at the back. He looked up at Carla. 'He will be OK,' he said. 'He's telling terrible jokes!' Carla smiled grimly. 'Orlando, there's a thick rope under that seat. Can you pass it to me, please?'

Orlando **dragged** the rope out. It was heavy, dirty, smelly and greasy. 'Ugh!' he muttered, but managed to drag the rope to the door. He **pushed** and

heaved it through the door, until it slid down to Cecil who let it fall to the floor before picking up one end.

Cecil attached the rope to the tractor, then threw the rest over the edge. He lowered himself down to the bush and could see the man's face now. He was obviously **VERY** cold because his skin was a pale white colour.

'Hi, my name is Cecil. What's yours?'

'Hello, Cecil. I'm Alex.' The man gasped, shivering. 'Pleased to meet you. Do I look bad?'

'You don't look pretty!' Cecil replied. 'But it looks as though you have two arms and two legs. That's a good start.'

Alex smiled. 'What do you want me to do?' he asked.

'Just lie still and I will dig you out, but you will have to do some walking. You're far too big for me to carry!' **They both laughed.** Cecil cleared the snow. 'How long have you been stuck here?' he asked.

'I don't know. What time is it now?' Alex answered.

'About half past eleven.'

'Then I've been trapped for about forty minutes.'

Ten minutes later, Cecil was bathed in sweat and Alex was free of the thorns. He tried to turn around and sit up but fell back in pain.

'Take it easy, Alex. Let me help you.'

'I won't argue with that,' Alex replied and Cecil helped him to sit up.

Together they managed to **scramble** back up the slope using the rope and Alex was soon squeezing into the cab of the warm tractor.

CARLA WAS OVERJOYED TO BE REUNITED WITH HER DADDY.

Cecil could not get in so he stood on the footplate. 'Now, Orlando, here's where you earn your corn,' he announced.

'Pardon?' replied Orlando. 'What do you mean?'

'That means it is time for you to do your job. Remember? The reason you came with me was to get a message to the caravan park down the hill.'

'Ah, yes,' said Orlando. 'But that was if there was an emergency.

'Correct, young man,' Cecil responded.

'But, there is no emergency now, is there?'

'No, there is no emergency but Alex here will need an ambulance. I think he has hypothermia or even frostbite and that will need treatment at the hospital.'

'I'll be OK, just as soon as I get warm again,' said Alex, but he was shivering violently.

'I hope so,' Cecil replied. 'Young Orlando is going to go down and get Pam to call for an ambulance. You need to see a doctor urgently.'

'Why don't you take him down in the tractor?' Orlando persisted. 'That would be much quicker.'

'For a start there ain't enough room for all of us and I'm not leaving you two children on the hill on your own, while I take him down.'

'I hadn't thought of that,' Orlando said. **THEN HE HAD AN IDEA.** 'We could sit in Alex's car and keep warm till you get back.'

'Not a chance!' Cecil countered. 'I'm worried that another vehicle could come round that top bend and crash into Alex's car at any moment. That would create a SERIOUS problem. It could even cause a disaster.'

They all looked at each other.

'Orlando, you're the only one who can do this now,' Cecil continued.

Grimly, Orlando agreed. 'OK, I'll go.'

Orlando smiled. This was going to be a *real-life* adventure. A proper mission – just like his dad undertakes every day in the SAS.

'That's my boy!' said Cecil. 'Tell them I am going to tow Alex's car down the hill and I should be there in about twenty minutes. The ambulance should be there by then.'

Orlando had never been on a sledge until this morning and, so far, had only travelled in a straight line. He did not know how to stop or how to make it turn, but this was his chance to do something **exciting!**

He was a little apprehensive, but climbed bravely out of the cab with Cecil's help. Gingerly he set the sledge down onto the snow-covered lane, holding the tow rope.

He looked down the slope and drew a deep breath when he spotted the sharp left-hand bend. **AND IT WAS VERY STEEP!**

The lane was not straight all the way down to the bend. It was curved like a banana to the right. That meant that the cliff was on his left and, if he did not follow the bend, he would be going over the side. **OVER THE EDGE. HE FROZE!**

'Just take it nice and steady, Orlando,' said Cecil. 'There's no rush. Just get down safely.'

'I will,' replied Orlando. He bent down to dip two fingers in the slushy mud at the side of the road. He drew the mud over one cheek under his eye just like an equal sign.

$$=$$

Then repeated this on his other cheek. **HE LOOKED JUST LIKE A SOLDIER GOING INTO BATTLE!**

Cecil saluted him. 'You won't have to worry about anything coming up the hill. Nothing can get up this bank 'cept my tractor. You'll be safe.'

I hope so! thought Orlando. **HE SQUATTED DOWN READY TO LIE ON HIS STOMACH**

ON THE SLEDGE.

'What are you doing, Orlando? Are you brilliant or just mad?' Cecil looked at him in disbelief.

Orlando was now on his knees by the side of the sledge. He looked at the farmer questioningly.

'You will fly down like an Olympic athlete like that. You'll be safer sitting up so you can use the turning and brake handles easier.'

Orlando looked **quizzically** at Cecil then at the sledge. He studied the two handles, one on either side and guessed that they must be what he was talking about.

'Oh, the brake handles,' he said nodding repeatedly. He sounded sure of himself. 'I wasn't going to use those. I was going to get down as fast as I could to save time. I like to go fast you see.'

'Yes, I see but I don't want you going and getting yourself killed! This slope is steep and it's very icy. If I were you, I would go down at a sensible speed.'

'OK. Why not?' said Orlando, sitting down on the sledge with one foot on either side in the snow.

Out of **SHEER** terror, he grabbed both of the

handles which seemed to give way and lifted up almost vertical. He looked at Cecil, then Carla and her dad.

'I'll see you all down at the bottom.' He looked down the hill with absolute **horror** but, fortunately, the others could not see his face. He could see the cliff edge!

He lifted his collar to his mouth and spoke quietly, 'Commando Orlando calling HQ, Commando Orlando calling HQ. Come in HQ.' He looked around. 'Commando Orlando from Task Force One about to commence Operation Arley Bank Rescue. Repeat. About to commence Operation Arley Bank Rescue. On my way down. On my way down.'

He looked down the slope. 'ETA dependant on unknown field conditions. Approximately three minutes. Repeat, three minutes. Over and out.'

'Bye,' he called.

Nothing happened.

'Bye,' they called back to him.

Nothing happened.

'Bye,' he repeated, this time realising that his feet were still on the snow. He lifted them onto the sledge and braced himself for the downward slide. **HE SQUEEZED HIS EYES TIGHT SHUT.**

'Bye,' they all repeated.

'Bye.'

Nothing happened.

'Are you going to release the brake handles or are you going to sit there all day?' Cecil asked.

'Pardon?' Orlando opened his eyes and looked at the handle in each hand. 'Oh.' He looked up at Cecil.

'I'm doing it slowly because this is a brand-new sledge and I am not sure how good they are,' he said, trying to show that he knew what he was talking about.

'If you release them any slower, you'll go backwards *up* the hill!' Cecil **laughed** and **winked** at the others. 'Remember, right handle to turn right and left handle to turn left.' Cecil scrutinised Orlando very carefully.

'Of course. Anyone knows that!' Orlando bluffed. He took a deep breath and **slowly** pushed the handles forward all the way. The sledge began to glide on the runners down the hill.

SLOWLY AT FIRST, THEN PICKING UP

SPEED.

Oh this is easy, thought Orlando, relieved somewhat.
The sledge moved faster...
And faster!

Until Orlando's eyes began to water with the cold wind. He blinked away the tears, then realised that the lane was bending away to his right. The tears streamed backwards to his ears. He looked like he was getting closer to the edge. He could hear Cecil's final words, 'Remember, right handle to go right and left handle to go left.'

He was sliding **perilously** close to the drop.

I certainly do not want to turn left now! he thought, so he pulled up the right handle and the sledge lurched away from the cliff.

He was now heading **fast** towards the other side of the lane – a huge bank of thorn bushes.

'Aaaarghh!'

he screamed and pulled up on the left handle.

The sledge headed towards the bushes, but slowed dramatically.

Orlando was learning; right handle to go right, left to go left, and both to slow down.

He released the right handle a little and the sledge turned straight down the middle of the road. He released both brakes and began to pick up speed again.

This was becoming fantastic!

Tears streamed over and under his ears. He **blinked** continuously to clear his vision and spotted the sharp left hand-bend. It was approaching like an express train.

He pulled gently up on both brakes to slow the sledge into the turn, then pulled up harder on the left brake. The sledge swung around the bend like a fighter plane at full throttle.

'Yeeeehaaa!' he screamed.

The next sixty seconds were the most exhilarating that Orlando had experienced in his life – **EVER!** Twisting and turning around the bends, he finally swung into the top entrance to the caravan park and brought his sledge to a halt in a swirl of snow right next to Pam's red van.

HE LIFTED HIS COLLAR AGAIN.
'Commando Orlando to Task Force. Orlando to Task Force. Operation Arley Bank Rescue. Down safe. Repeat, down safe. Perimeter secure and no sign of hostiles. Just going inside. Out.'

One hour later everybody was saying their goodbyes to Alex and Carla. They watched as the ambulance took them away.

Arthur and Margaret were still looking after Sylvester and Tyrone. Ma had joined them with Beyonsay and Channing because Arthur had called her to tell her what had happened.

Jeffrey and Cordelia, the caravan park owners, brought out some hot chocolate.

'Ooh, Carla would have loved this!' said Cecil. 'She doesn't like tea!'

'I'll save her some,' said Jeffrey.

'It'll be *cold chocolate* by then!' Cecil called out,

laughing, and swung up into his tractor. Pam **jumped** into her red van and they both drove off in opposite directions.

'Come on,' said Ma. 'Let's go and have some lunch. Then we can all go up the hill and do some sledging.'

'Yeah!' they all yelled.

'And Orlando,' Ma added. 'You can get those dirty marks off your face!'

Orlando saluted and spoke into his collar. 'Over and out,' he whispered.

CHAPTER FIFTEEN
Rolling in the Deep

The children were sitting around the kitchen table. Lunch was beans on toast with grated cheese, followed by fresh blueberries and yoghurt.

Orlando and Sylvester exchanged a glance, both remembering how **painful** it felt when Arthur had catapulted frozen blueberries at them a few days ago.

Ma's phone rang. They all looked up.

'Hello,' she answered.

''Ello,' burbled Beyonsay, mimicking her mother. She banged her spoon on her tray, laughing.

All the children laughed loudly.

'Shhh!' Ma hissed, smiling with them.

'Sorry! Pardon? Could you say that again? The

children got a bit excited just then.' She waited. 'Yes,' she said.

Sylvester mouthed to Orlando, *'Who is that?'*

Orlando shrugged. *'No idea!'* he mouthed back.

There was a long pause before Ma spoke again.

'Oh yes. How are they?'

The children listened intently, straining to hear the person at the other end of the phone.

Channing mouthed, *'It could be the hospital.'*

'Good I'm so glad to hear that,' Ma added. 'Left something? . . . Wouldn't say.'

THE CHILDREN STARED AT MA.

Orlando whispered, 'There was *nothing* left when they went to the hospital. Arthur put their bags in the ambulance.'

'Well, we're going sledging after lunch. We could collect it on our way up the bank,' said Ma.

'Collect *what*?' Sylvester said with a hiss.

'Dunno,' Orlando replied softly. 'Nothing to collect.'

'Thank you for letting me know.' Ma turned her phone off. 'That was Cordelia from the caravan park.

234

Alex and Carla have been cleared by the doctor and Alex has just driven off home. She said that he has left something for Orlando at her house.'

'What is it?' Sylvester chirped.

'She would not say, but asked for us to call in and she will present it to him.'

'Present it? Oh, that sounds official,' Channing declared. 'I wonder what it could be.'

'I bet it's a new catapult,' Sylvester suggested.

'No chance!' Channing replied laughing. 'It's probably a bag of sweets from the Olde Sweet Shoppe in Bingham.'

'Or a bar of chocolate,' Tyrone said, joining in.

'Chocrat,' said Beyonsay giggling, and they all laughed.

'It might be a certificate of commendation,' Sylvester said.

Orlando pulled a face at him as if to say *why do I need a certificate?*

Half an hour later, after the washing up had been done and the crockery put away, everyone was standing outside the front door in deep snow waiting, while Ma sat Beyonsay safely onto Orlando's sledge.

'Now, hold on tightly with both hands,' she said. 'And don't fidget or you will fall off.'

'Fall off,' Beyonsay copied.

Everyone was wearing their WARMEST coats, scarfs, gloves and wellies with several pairs of socks, but it still felt cold – an icy cold that froze their cheeks!

'Shall we go up the path through the woods or up the lane?' asked Ma.

'It will be too difficult through the woods pulling Beyonsay,' Orlando replied. 'Besides, there could be hostiles hiding behind any tree ready to capture us.' He looked at Sylvester and nodded, grimly. **THE WAY THE SOLDIERS DO IN FILMS.**

Channing looked at Ma and they both laughed. 'You two are mad,' she scoffed.

The boys picked up their sticks from the side of the house and held them **COMMANDO** style.

'Let's move out,' Orlando ordered and led the way down the drive in deep, fresh snow, with Sylvester at his side. They both surveyed the hedges and fields on their own side in a well-practised manoeuvre.

'Are we going to have this all afternoon, lads?' Ma asked, resigned.

Channing pulled Beyonsay along while Ma and Tyrone dragged the other two empty sledges.

'You know you won't get any sense out of them now, Ma,' Channing mocked.

They noticed that the pond was covered in ice. Sylvester picked up a small stick and threw it into the middle. The stick bounced off and slid all the way to the other side of the pond with a scraping sound.

'Wow! That must be thick,' he guessed.

Channing seized her chance. 'Not as thick as you!' she barked.

Sylvester turned to attack but Ma spoke first. 'Not as thick as you – *might expect*,' she added cleverly.

Sylvester was ready to erupt, but this CALMED him down. He turned to scan the fields again. Channing **smirked.**

'And don't you two go thinking that you can walk on that ice. It will not be strong enough to take your weight. Do you understand?'

NOTHING.

The boys peered into hedges.

'Are you two soldiers listening to me?' she roared.

'*Commandos*, Ma. *Commandos*, not soldiers,' Orlando corrected her.

'You'll get a clip, Orlando! Do you understand me?'

'Yes, Ma. Don't go on the ice,' Orlando recited and gave one of his looks to Sylvester. Channing spotted it and knew exactly what it meant – later they would be going on the ice! **THAT, SHE WOULD HAVE TO SEE!**

It was hard work trudging up the hill in the snow, but at least they were no longer cold. Except for Beyonsay. She began to cry and Ma picked her up.

Channing now pulled two sledges, but it was not long before they came to the caravan park. The two commandos headed for the main house where Jeffrey and Cordelia lived.

THE LODGE

Orlando **knocked** the door then stood back to let Ma through. He turned to stand next to Sylvester, one on each side of the porch facing back down the path, scanning for **HOSTILES**. They held their 'guns' across their chests in readiness.

CHANNING TITTERED AND MA TOOK NO NOTICE.

The door opened and a smiling Cordelia welcomed them. 'Come in,' she said, opening the door wide.

'Leave the sledges outside,' Ma said. 'And the assault rifles.'

'Pants!' muttered Orlando.

'Rifles?' Cordelia queried. 'Are we expecting trouble?' she smiled at Ma.

'It's just their little game,' Channing taunted.

'They're playing commandos,' Ma added, smiling weakly.

'Yes. Just like Dad,' Orlando revealed. 'He's in the SAS.'

'Shh, that's enough now!' Ma whispered.

'That sounds exciting,' Cordelia said, looking at Orlando.

'No, it's not because we never see him,' he said despairingly.

Cordelia caught Ma's expression and decided to leave the rest of that conversation for another time. She led the way through into the lounge where everyone sat down.

'OK,' she announced, 'as you know, there was quite a serious incident up on the hill today.'

Jeffrey came in carrying a tray full of drinks. 'Alex and Carla came back to let us know they were safe and well, and Alex left this envelope for you Orlando. He wanted to say *thank you* for your help.'

Jeffrey put the tray down and handed the envelope to Orlando.

He turned it over and it read:

To Orlando – with thanks.

He stared at it for a long time. **SPEECHLESS.**

'Well, are you going to open it, young man?' Cordelia asked, breaking the silence. She offered him a small knife.

'I thought this would be a little safer than using your bayonet,' she added, smiling at Ma. Orlando gazed at it.

'It's for opening letters,' she said.

'Oh, yes,' Orlando took it from her and carefully slit open the envelope.

EVERYONE STARED INTENTLY AS HE PULLED OUT A CARD.

On the front was a snow scene and, in large blue letters, were the words: Thank you!

Orlando studied it for a while and held it up for the others to see. Then he slowly opened it. And something dropped out and landed on his lap. He looked down in disbelief.

IT WAS A

£10 NOTE.

'*Wow*!' shouted Sylvester.

'What is it?' Tyrone asked.

'It's a ten-pound note!' Sylvester responded.

Ma smiled. Channing was **flabbergasted.**

Beyonsay clapped. 'Den down oat,' she gurgled.

Everyone laughed.

Orlando began to read the message inside.

'What does it say?' Jeffrey asked.

'Read it out, Orlando,' Ma encouraged.

Orlando spoke:

> To Orlando,
>
> Carla and I want to say a great big thank
> you to a very kind and brave boy. Without
> your help we might still be stuck on the hill.
> I hope you can find something to spend this
> on. You were amazing!
>
> Love from Alex and Carla.
> xx
>
> H Q - over and out!

'He *heard* me!' Orlando spluttered, embarrassed.

Everyone laughed.

Orlando looked around and joined in, holding up his ten-pound note. Little did he know that this would not be his **ONLY** shock of the day.

'We're going sledging now,' he told them.

'Would you like to come and join us?' Ma asked Cordelia and Jeffrey.

'No, thank you. Not for me.' Jeffrey breathed in loudly. 'I've got to clear piles of snow from the footpaths.'

'I think I will give it a miss too,' replied Cordelia. 'The last time I went sledging, I ended up landing on my bottom and broke my coccyx!' She looked at Ma and they both laughed.

Twenty minutes later, tired and exhausted from the climb, everybody arrived at the top of the hill and looked down. They could see woods behind Arthur and Margaret's house and, further down, they could make out part of their garden and cottage. Beyond that they could see the pond.

IT WAS A MASSIVE HILL AND STEEP IN PLACES.

They could see for miles and, as far as they could see down the valley, there was no colour showing.

Only black or white. It was a strange, **amazing** sight.

'Now,' said Ma. 'Let's be careful and sensible. We don't want to go all the way down. It'll be torture getting back up. We can go *all* the way down on our last run. What do you say?'

'Sounds good to me, Ma,' agreed Channing.

'And me,' said Orlando and Sylvester in unison.

'Me too,' said Tyrone, joining in.

'Me, me, me, me, me!' Beyonsay giggled, **clapping** her hands enthusiastically.

'Good. We'll head towards that bush, about forty metres away. Can you see it?' said Ma.

They all nodded and the next twenty minutes were amazing. Orlando showed them how the brakes worked and how to turn the sledge. They all soon got the hang of it and the children were **IMPRESSED** with Ma, whose turns were very controlled.

'Ma, you look like an expert,' Sylvester observed

'I love it!' Ma replied. 'Except the walking back up! I'll need something stronger than a cup of tea after this.'

She sat Beyonsay in her lap and took her down

several times, while the baby giggled with delight each time.

'Can *I* take Beyonsay down, Ma?' Channing asked.

'Yes, but please go very slowly,' Ma replied.

Ma was very nervous at first, but realised that Channing was sensible and capable.

Orlando and Sylvester began to argue over who would be next to take her down.

'Stop squabbling you two and take it in turns, or you will not be taking anyone down.'

While they took turns with Beyonsay, Tyrone began to roll a snowball and, when it became too big for him to push, Ma helped him. It soon became a huge Snowball!

'I know!' shouted Orlando. 'Let's build a snowman.'

Sylvester began to sing *Do you wanna build a snowman?*

'Just like the one you built for Mrs Chisholm in school yesterday?' Channing remarked sarcastically.

That took the smile off Orlando's face, but he was not intimidated.

'No,' he answered. **'BIGGER!'**

From then onwards, when they were not sledging, they helped to build a bigger snowman.

Just then, as if from nowhere, Arthur and Margaret arrived with Floss. Both had a long, THIN bag strapped on their backs, which they laid on the floor.

'We wanted to see what all the noise was about,' said Arthur with a cheerful laugh.

Ma was flying down the hill, having a race with Tyrone and Sylvester. Floss took off after them, leapt on Sylvester when he **jumped** off at the end of the run, and they both went rolling over and over in the snow. Everyone laughed.

Floss **SNEEZED** and began to chomp at the snow. Arthur **laughed**. 'Don't eat any yellow snow, Floss!' he called out.

'Floss absolutely loves the snow,' said Margaret. 'And I can see you are all having a wonderful time.'

'We're having a great time, Margaret, thank you. What's in those bags?' Channing asked.

'Those are our skis. We are going to ski back down the lane when we go home.'

'Skis! That must be fun,' Channing said. 'I've never

been skiing, but I've seen it on the telly. They go very fast, don't they?'

'We don't go quite as fast as *they* do, Channing,' Arthur **chuckled.** 'Not at our age!'

Ma arrived back at the top. She was slightly out of breath. 'Hello, you two. I'm glad you've come to join us. Would you like a go on the sledge?' she asked Arthur and Margaret.

'I would love a go,' Arthur replied.

'Oh, not for me,' said Margaret. 'I think I'll stick to my skiing! I'll watch you lot enjoying yourselves.'

Arthur sat on the sledge and let go of the brakes. He **turned** and **twisted** his way down the slope like an expert.

'Wow, look at Artur the Fartur go!' yelled Sylvester, as Arthur flew past him on his way back up with Floss.

'Go, Artur!' called Channing.

'Arty farty!' called Beyonsay.

Floss **BARKED** and sped off after Arthur down the hill. She leapt on him before he could even get off the sledge and they both ROLLED further down the slope. Arthur was laughing uncontrollably.

"Ere, where's Budleigh Cottage?' said a voice behind them. 'It's around 'ere somewhere, ain't it?' the voice continued.

Ma and Margaret were standing together watching Arthur and Floss. All the children were busy adding snow to the snowman, except for Sylvester who was almost back up at the start of the sledge run.

Everyone turned to look up at a man in a blue, one-piece overall. He was not big – he was colossal, and bald, and he stood looking down at them. He was flanked by two other men, equal in size and wearing the same blue outfits. **THEY WERE THE BIGGEST MEN THAT THE CHILDREN HAD EVER SEEN.**

Ma was the first to respond. 'I'm sorry, what did you say?' The man spoke slowly and deliberately as though he needed to think about every word. 'I said, do you know–'

He was cut off by the man on his right, 'Malcolm wants to know where Budleigh Cottage is. Could you help us? Do you happen to know, please?' The man was very quietly spoken and looked kindly at them.

Arthur **staggered** up, breathless, dragging the sledge with Floss riding on it. 'What's happening?' he asked, looking at Margaret and Ma and the three men.

'I'm sorry,' the man continued. 'How bad mannered of me. Please let me introduce us. My name is Duttan. I'm from Zimbabwe,' he grinned magnificently and carried on, 'the most beautiful country in the whole of Africa.'

He pointed to the bald man in the middle. 'This is Malcolm and this,' he pointed at the man on the other side of Malcolm, 'is Perry–'

'It's not Perry. I keep telling you! My name is Sebastian,' said the third man.

'Leave it out, Perry!' shouted Malcolm. 'You know it *is* Perry.'

'I changed it, didn't I?' Perry whined. 'Sebastian sounds much better for a–'

'I know where it is,' interrupted Tyrone.

EVERYONE STOPPED AND TURNED TO LOOK AT THE LITTLE VOICE.

'It's down there.' He pointed down the hill.

'You what?' said Malcolm.

'It's that house at the bottom by the trees.'

The three men looked down to where Tyrone pointed. 'Budleigh Cottage,' he added.

'I say, do you mean *that* house down there is actually Budleigh Cottage?' asked Duttan.

No one spoke.

'That means we gotta go down that lane all the way 'round this hill to get there,' said Perry.

'I ain't driving that van down that lane, Duttan! It's too dangerous!' said Malcolm, the bald man. 'I ain't getting killed for nobody.'

'Maybe we won't have to,' said Duttan thoughtfully. 'Come with me.'

He quickly **plodded** through the snow down towards Ma and the others.

'Wait for me,' called Malcolm, who stepped down and immediately slipped onto his backside and skidded sideways into the back of Duttan's legs. *'Piddlesticks!'* he screamed.

'Knickers!' yelled Duttan, and they both slid down in a heap to Ma's feet.

Perry fell forward and slid all the way down on his

stomach like a surfboard and HAMMERED into the two of them. *'Cocklesticks!'* he roared.

Duttan stood up and turned to Perry. 'Go and get the boss,' he ordered.

Perry stood up and turned to Malcolm. 'Go and get the boss,' he commanded.

Malcolm stood up and immediately lost his footing. His legs shot up into the air and he landed on his big bottom on the snow once more.

'Would you mind awfully if we borrowed your sledges to get down the hill, please?' Duttan enquired.

It was not really a question and, before anyone could stop them, they had **GRABBED** the three sledges, pushing Arthur over in the snow in the process. Floss began to **bark** and GROWL. Margaret and Ma helped him get back to his feet.

'I ain't never been on one of these before,' Malcolm said.

'Shut up and sit down. Just aim it at that house down there,' Perry instructed.

'Are you sure this is easy?'

'Like falling off a log. Now belt up and get moving!'

Perry ordered.

'Will you two please be quiet and get on with it?' Duttan complained.

THEY ALL SAT ON A SLEDGE AND PUSHED OFF.

They began slowly at first due to their extra weight but after a few metres, they began to pick up speed, getting faster and faster, until it was obvious they were not going to stop until they reached America or hit something big!

The men did not know about the brakes and were totally out of control.

'Blimey! Where's the brakes?' Malcolm bellowed. He screamed. A long, agonising, scream.

Then...

'Mummy! I want my mummeeeeee!'

THEY COULD HEAR HIM BACK AT THE TOP OF THE HILL.

The three men were now travelling so fast that their eyes were watering and they could not see a thing.

Duttan closed his eyes completely and yelled, 'Umiguli!'

'Suffering sausages!' screamed Perry. *'Duttan, if I survive this you can call me Perry as much as you like!'*

'If we survive this, Perry, you can call me Auntie Mary!'

Just before the hedge around the garden of Budleigh Cottage there was a hump.

All three of them hit the HUMP and took off, airborne, just like ski jumpers in the Olympics. All three of them were screaming now.

'Geronimo!'

'UMIGULI!'

'Knikkersnikker!'

The sledges came back down to earth on the other side of the hedge and careered headlong towards the pond. In front of the pond there was a row of bricks that edged the footpath. All three sledges hit the bricks head on and came to an immediate stop.

THE MEN DID NOT!

'I want my rubber ring!'

The three men became airborne for a second time with arms and legs **thrashing** wildly, as they soared spectacularly through the air to come **_crashing_** down in the middle of the pond, face down, side by side.

They smashed through the ice and disappeared.

At the top of the hill, everyone watched in amused horror.

'We won't be able to go on the ice now, Sylvester!' Orlando observed miserably.

EVERYONE SCANNED THE ICY SURFACE IN SILENCE.

The pond settled for several seconds then, all at once, the three men sat up gasping for air. Malcolm sneezed so loudly they could hear him at the top.

'I guess they'll need a hot bath and some dry clothes,' said a voice behind them.

They all turned around to find a tall, slender man in the same blue uniform as the three huge men. He was some thirty metres away looking down at them and smiling.

There was a long pause during which no one spoke.

*

Arthur and Margaret smiled politely at the man but did not recognise him.

THE SHUFFLETTS STARED AT THE MAN IN DISBELIEF.

The man continued to smile, and then held out his arms. Arthur looked hard at the man and back at Ma and the children. Their faces seemed suspended in stunned silence.

There's something strange going on here, he thought.

Ma put her hand to her mouth and gasped. '*Mick,*' she whispered.

'*Dad?*' said Channing questioningly.

'Dad,' mumbled Sylvester thoughtfully. Then, more confidently, 'It's Dad!'

Orlando was not listening. He was on his way up the hill, **scrambling** hard through the snow, sliding, slipping, skidding, straining and gasping for breath.

'DAD!' he yelled.

'Dad!' He had waited a long time for this moment.' Dad!' he shrieked again.

He threw himself into his father's open arms like a ragdoll, tears streaming down his cheeks. They both fell over, rolling in the deep snow at the side of the road, **laughing.**

CHAPTER SIXTEEN
Surprise, Surprise

Dad scooped snow into Orlando's face and roared with glee as Orlando squealed.

Seconds later, Channing and Sylvester arrived and dived on top, and all four of them were **hugging** and SQUEEZING and rolling in the snow, pushing handfuls at each other. Floss appeared from nowhere and began jumping on top of them all.

'That's their dad, Arthur,' Margaret muttered quietly.

'Yes, I gathered that,' Arthur replied. 'But I know his face from somewhere.'

Dad dragged himself out from underneath the pile onto his knees and scooped up more snow and threw it over everybody.

They were all **screaming** and **squirming** at the cold snow in their faces.

Arthur and Margaret looked on. 'I'm sure I've seen him before – many times, but I can't think where.' Arthur was puzzled.

'It will come to you, Arthur. Just give it time,' Margaret responded.

'Daddy.'

Dad felt a tap on his shoulder.

'Daddy.'

Dad turned around to see Tyrone standing right next to him.

'Daddy, I missed you,' said Tyrone and he leapt into his father's arms and SQUEEZED him tightly.

Fighting back the tears, Mick **HUGGED** his youngest son. He looked up just in time to see Ma and Beyonsay reach the top of the slope, helped by Arthur and Margaret.

'Becky,' he said. Scooping up Tyrone, he stood up and ran to them. Beyonsay and Tyrone disappeared in the middle of a **COLOSSAL** hug between Ma and Dad.

Arthur studied the sign on the white van.

Maybe it would give him a clue as to where he had seen this man before. He read the large letters but could not read the smaller words without his glasses. The van looked clean apart from the dirty **BLACK** snow, which had sprayed up from the wheels. He wondered why an SAS soldier would be driving around in a laundry van. He turned to look back at Dad. He was kissing Ma. Beyonsay and Tyrone were **STRUGGLING** to get out from between them.

Dad put Tyrone carefully down onto the snow and reached for Beyonsay, but she turned her head away to cling on tightly around Ma's neck.

'She doesn't recognise you, Mick. Remember, she

has never seen you before. You're a stranger to her! I'm sorry.'

Beyonsay clung on **firmly** around Ma's neck with both arms.

Mick looked **DEVASTATED**. 'Oh come on, baby. Please give Daddy a hug.' Beyonsay snuggled hard in to Ma's neck, turning her back on her dad.

'I have waited a long time to see you, my little precious girl,' he added, but there was still no response from Beyonsay.

Ma looked at him sadly and gave a gentle shake of her head. 'Leave her for now,' she whispered. 'She doesn't know who you are.'

Mick looked DESOLATE but nodded. 'OK,' he said.

He looked around at everybody. 'We'd better go and get my three amigos from out of that lake before they freeze to death. Which is the best way off this mountain?'

ORLANDO TOOK CHARGE. 'We would be better going straight down the hill, Dad, the way your friends—' He stopped mid-sentence with a look of concern on his face. 'Are *they* your *friends*?' he asked incredulously.

Dad thought carefully, searching for the right words. 'They are my *minders*,' he replied, 'my... *security*. They look after me and keep me safe.'

'Wow!' said Sylvester. 'You must be important to have your own security guards!'

Dad smiled. 'Come on,' he said holding out his arms, 'let's get going before *we* all freeze to death!'

Tyrone took hold of his dad's hand and Channing **grabbed** his other arm tightly. Sylvester joined Tyrone.

'Will everybody be OK going down this way?' Dad asked, looking around. 'It's very steep!'

'We brought our skis with us, so we will go back down the lane,' Arthur replied. 'The way we came up.' He passed a ski bag to Margaret. She opened it to reveal skis and ski poles.

'They look amazing,' said Orlando. 'Is it easy to ski?'

'Yes, when you know how,' Margaret replied. 'We have been skiing for many years.'

'You do a lot of falling over when you are learning though!' Arthur laughed. 'I know, *I* did.'

'But we will get down a lot faster than we came up!' Margaret added, chuckling. 'If you like, Becky, we can ski back to *your* cottage and get the kettle on.'

'That would be fabulous,' said Ma. 'I think it will take us about twenty minutes to walk down. We will have to take great care.'

'No it won't, Ma,' said Orlando with a grin. 'We can take the easy way.'

'What's the easy way?' she asked.

'Sliding down on our bums!'

Orlando took Beyonsay from Ma and put her on his lap as he sat down on the snow.

'All you do now is . . . s s s l i d e. Bye!'

AND OFF HE SLID.

Beyonsay squealed with delight, even though they were not going anywhere near as fast as they did on the sledges.

'Orlando to HQ. Orlando to HQ. On our way. ETA ten minutes.'

'We will see you down there, Becky, Mick,' Arthur

called as he clipped his heels into his skis. 'Are you ready, Margaret?'

'I certainly am,' she said with a smile, and off they went, swishing their way down the snowy lane. Floss skidded and slid and leapt behind them.

The children **waved** and, linking arms, they sat down with Dad to begin the **BUM** slide. Ma joined them and they all sat in a straight line to begin the countdown.

FIVE

    FOUR

        THREE

            TWO

                ONE

                    GO!

When they finally reached the cottage, they found Arthur and Margaret in the kitchen making hot drinks and soup.

'Where are my men?' Dad asked, looking around.

'They are in the lounge,' Arthur answered.

'Where is the lounge?' Dad asked.

'It's this way,' Sylvester responded. 'Follow me, Dad.'

He opened the door to the lounge and led Dad inside. The three men were sat on chairs leaning as close to the log burner as possible.

Sylvester could see some flames behind the glass but, in spite of this, the men were shivering and dithering. There was STEAM coming off their clothes and they all had green slime on them.

'They are too close to the fire, Dad. Look! They are on fire!' he cried.

Dad laughed and replied, 'No, they aren't on fire. They're *steaming.*'

They looked a sorry state, **shaking** and trying to warm their hands against the fire. Their teeth and jaws were all chattering so much they looked like puppets.

They turned around when the door opened.

'Ere B-B-Boss, w-w-what are we g-g-g-gonna do? I'm f-f-freezing to d-d-d-d-death 'ere.'

'Quiet, Malcolm and let me think,' Dad retorted. 'Sylvester, you go and help your Ma,' he said, ushering Sylvester out and closing the door behind him.

In the kitchen Ma took charge. She was not sure how this would work out.

'OK,' she said to the children. 'Everyone upstairs to get changed. Come on. Quickly! Get those wet clothes off and into the laundry bin. When you're nice and dry, come down here for some lovely soup that Margaret has made.'

THEY ALL KICKED OFF THEIR WELLIES AND RAN UPSTAIRS.

'Channing, bring me some clean clothes and a nappy for Beyonsay. I'll change her down here,' Ma called.

She spotted Sylvester coming out of the lounge. 'Sylvester. Ask Orlando to bring me six of the biggest towels he can find, please. Help him if he needs help. OK?'

'Righty oh, Ma,' he shouted back. 'Who are tho—'

'Not now, Sylvester. *Move it*!'

MA WENT BACK INTO THE KITCHEN.

'Becky, can you tell us what is going on? That man

is your husband, Mick, yes? But who are the others?' Arthur enquired.

'I wish I knew, Arthur,' she answered thoughtfully. 'I wish I knew.'

'They need to get out of those wet clothes or they will end up with pneumonia,' Margaret spoke kindly, stirring the soup.

'Yes, I know,' Becky responded. 'I've sent for towels for them and we will have to get their clothes dried.'

She left them to the food preparations and opened the door into the lounge.

Quietly, but firmly, she whispered, 'Mick, I need to talk to you.'

HE LOOKED BACK AT HER. THE MEN LOOKED AT MICK THEN AT BECKY.

'Mick?' Perry queried. 'Who's Mick?'

'*NOW*!' Becky hissed.

'Who's Mick, 'Arry?' Malcolm looked confused. But it did not take much to confuse Malcolm at any time.

MICK TURNED TO FOLLOW BECKY.

'Harry, who is Mick?' Duttan asked Mick softly.

Mick looked back at him and said, 'I'll explain later. Just wait here.' He closed the door behind him and stood in the hall looking at Becky, waiting for the inevitable questions.

Just then, Orlando came scurrying down the stairs carrying an armful of towels with Sylvester behind carrying two more. Tyrone was right behind Sylvester holding a nappy and Channing followed them both with Beyonsay's clothes. They all stood in a line staring at Ma and Dad. The inevitable questions would have to wait.

Ma took the towels and gave them to Dad. 'Give your mates two each and bring them up to the bathrooms where they can have a shower and get cleaned up. Follow me.'

Ma looked at the children. 'Now, go into the kitchen and help Arthur and Margaret with the drinks and food and don't ask any questions. Do you understand?' She gave them '*the look*'.

'Yes, Ma,' they replied.

Mick opened the door to the lounge and began to bellow orders.

'Right you lot. Move it. Grab two towels each and follow me upstairs!'

The three men DRIPPED dirty water everywhere as they followed Becky and Mick.

She showed them to the family bathroom. 'Malcolm – you're in here,' Mick instructed.

'Bring your wet clothes downstairs when you're finished and we will try to get them clean and dry,' Ma added.

'What am I gonna wear?' Malcolm moaned.

'Well I've got nothing anywhere near your size...' Mick was cut off.

'Come down wearing those two towels and sit by the fire,' Becky barked. She was in no mood for an argument. 'You will have to wear *them* until your clothes are ready.'

'I ain't—'

'Malcolm! Shut it!' said Mick, and Becky gave him a very curious glance. She had never heard him speak like that before.

'Sorry, 'Arry,' he muttered.

She led the way to the en-suite in Channing's room.

'Duttan, you can go in here, and bring...'

'Bring my wet clothes down. Yes, I know, Harry.'

He looked at Becky and added. 'Thank you so much for looking after us lads, Mrs Daykins. We really do appreciate your kindness.'

Becky looked at Mick, but said nothing and led the way to the en-suite in her own room.

'Perry. You're in here and don't forget to bring all your wet clothes down for cleaning,' Dad reminded.

'No probs, 'Arry,' he responded. 'Oh, 'Arry please would mind calling me Sebastian in front of the other lads. You know I prefer it.'

'Will do, Perry!' Mick said with a laugh. 'I mean, Sebastian.' He nodded and gave a wink.

'Fanks, 'Arry. I won't be long. See you downstairs.'

'See you downstairs, Sebastian.'

Sebastian **grinned.**

In the kitchen, the children were laying crockery and

cutlery, with Channing and Orlando spreading butter on bread.

'Your children are very helpful, Becky,' Margaret admired. 'They know just what to do, don't they, Arthur?'

'They are well-trained, Margaret,' Ma smiled. 'Thank you. What do you say to Margaret, children?'

'Thank you, Margaret,' they chorused. Ma always liked them to say '*Thank you*' to anyone who gave them a compliment.

Dad arrived in the kitchen. 'It's lovely and warm in here,' he said. 'Now, what can I do to help?' He moved from Orlando to Channing, Tyrone to Sylvester giving each of them hugs and squeezes. Beyonsay saw him coming and turned away towards Ma. He left her alone, disappointedly.

'If I go and build the fire up, could you get some more logs from just outside the door from the log store?' Arthur said.

Dad finished the hugs and disappeared outside and Arthur went into the lounge to add more logs to the fire so the men would be warm, then the children sat down to eat. Ma left the kitchen door very slightly ajar, listening for the men returning to the lounge.

'Becky, I'm a bit worried. What *is* going on?' Margaret said softly.

'I will tell you just as soon as I get some answers myself, Margaret,' Ma replied.

Upstairs, Duttan was ready first. He **squeezed** the remaining dirty water out of his clothes into the sink and rolled them together in one bundle. He wore one towel around his waist and the other around his shoulders.

He was now sitting on the top stair waiting for the other two.

Malcolm appeared. ''Ere, Duttan, what 'ave you done wiv your clothes?'

'Wring them out in the sink and roll them into a ball, then bring them here,' Duttan replied.

Malcolm disappeared and Sebastian came **shuffling** along the landing, **SINGING**. He was wearing his two towels just like Duttan and carried his clothes in a bundle but, under his towels, he wore a frilly pink dressing gown that was miles too small for him. It was so tight that he could hardly move and he had split it in several places.

On his head he wore Ma's flowery shower cap and on his feet, he sported a pair of Ma's pink mule slippers. Most of each foot splayed outside the slipper, but Sebastian seemed very pleased. He sang into a hand-held hairbrush, *'I Want to Break Free.'*

'Very nice,' said Duttan.

'Thanks, Dutt. Do you like my singing then?'

'No. I was talking about your clothes!'

'I think pink suits me, don't you? What's happening, Dutt?' he enquired.

'Just waiting for Malcolm, Perry. Sorry... Sebastian!'

Sebastian grinned.

Malcolm arrived and they all went downstairs. They looked a strange bunch, dressed in almost nothing but two towels and, being very big men, the towels only just fitted.

Duttan stopped at the partly-open kitchen door. He coughed exaggeratedly and called, 'Hello. Mrs

Daykins, are you there? We've got our dirty clothes here for you.'

The door **SWUNG** open and Becky stood looking at them. She stared at Sebastian wearing her clothes, but decided to say nothing.

Behind her, Mick had an armful of logs. He looked at them and *he* could *not* help himself. He laughed uncontrollably.

''Ere wotchu laughing at, 'Arry?' Malcolm looked confused.

Malcolm was like an enormous Humpty Dumpty. He was completely bald and did not seem to have a neck. Instead, his whole body started at the top of his egg-shaped head and became **WIDER** and **WIDER** all the way down to his legs, which looked like two stalks.

''Arry. Stop laughin'.'

Duttan smiled. 'Where would you like us to put our clothes?'

'Follow me,' said Becky, and she led them through the kitchen to the laundry room.

In total silence, everyone watched the three huge

men plod barefoot through the kitchen. The only sound was the flopping of Sebastian's slippers.

Malcolm hit his head on the light bulb with a **'PING'** and the children sniggered.

'Ow!' he yelled as the hot bulb burned his forehead.

Mick laughed again and took the pile of logs through to the lounge.

In the laundry room, Becky pointed to the washing machine. 'Drop them on the floor there,' she directed. The men did as they were told and stepped back just as Mick returned.

'Now, Mick. I mean, *Harry*, get them back into the lounge in front of the fire before they catch their death.'

Malcolm managed to **BANG** his head on the lightbulb on the way back and had a burn mark on each side of his forehead.

'Looks like the light's on but there is no one at home!' Arthur said with a chuckle. Margaret laughed.

Becky could not hold it any longer and **burst** out laughing.

CHAPTER SEVENTEEN
Let's Stick Together

As soon as the children's dad, Mick, had closed the lounge door, the three men **bounced** questions at him.

Duttan spoke first. 'Harry, what is going on?' he said.

'Yeah, like wassapenin'?' said Malcolm.

Sebastian looked confused. 'We know this is your family, right, but why does she keep calling you 'Mick'?' he said.

'Let's sit down and I'll explain,' Mick said, pulling up a chair to join the three around the log fire.

Once settled, Mick took a **DEEP** breath. 'It's difficult to know where to start.'

'Look, Harry,' Duttan cut in. 'You are our boss.

We have known you for a long time as the man everybody in prison fears and respects. When you say *"Get something done"* it gets done.'

'Yeah,' Malcolm joined in. 'You tell me to squeeze somebody and I squeeze 'em and they squeal. Nobody don't ask no questions 'cos you're the boss.'

'We look after you, 'Arry, 'cos you look after us,' Sebastian added.

'I know that, lads and I appreciate it. I don't know where I would be without you lads to look after me. Prison is not a hotel.'

'You get us extra food,' Sebastian continued.

'And comics,' Malcolm added.

'And football on the telly.'

'And comics.'

'And salad cream. I like salad cream on my chips,' Sebastian said appreciatively.

'And comics. I like the pictures,' said Malcolm with a smile.

'Stop,' Duttan held up both hands. 'Stop. We know he helps us. He's our boss. He makes the decisions, protects us from the screws (*warders) and gets us everything we need. That's why we protect him. Now get a grip and calm down.'

THEY ALL LOOKED AT MICK INTENTLY.

He took another long breath. 'You see, my real name *is* Mick. Mick Shufflett and I am a taxi driver. I'm not a bank robber or a villain of any sort.

HE WAITED FOR THE REACTION.

'You mean you ain't 'Arry, 'Arry?' said Malcolm.

MICK SHOOK HIS HEAD.

'You're not 'Arry 'Crusher' Daykins, the gang leader?' Sebastian probed.

HE SHOOK HIS HEAD AGAIN.

'You're 'avin' a big fat giraffe, ain't ya?' Malcolm

said, and he began to laugh loudly.

MICK HUNG HIS HEAD.

There was a long silence during which the three minders exchanged many looks and glances. It was Duttan who spoke next.

'Let me get this correct, Harry. Sorry, Mick. I say, do you mind if I continue to call you Harry? It just seems so right.'

MICK NODDED.

'So, Harry, you are not the feared gangster that we all thought you were? All this time in prison you've had us fooled. You've tricked us! Can I ask *why*?'

MICK LIFTED HIS HEAD SLOWLY.

'It wasn't my idea.' He gazed at the fire, saying nothing.

THE THREE MEN LOOKED AT HIM, STARING, WAITING FOR AN ANSWER.

'Whose idea was it then, 'Arry?' Sebastian asked.

'It was the warden's idea all along,' he responded.

'The warden?' Duttan intervened. 'Do you mean the warden of Moldham prison?'

'Yes, that's exactly who I mean. Warden Banks. It

was his idea all along. You see, when they took me into the prison they realised that I looked exactly like Harry Daykins, the gangster. I don't mean just a bit like him. We look like twins. We are *identical*.'

'Cor blimey, 'Arry,' Malcolm grunted.

'Oh my giddy aunt!' Sebastian mumbled.

'So what happened next?' Duttan continued.

'Well, Harry Daykins was being moved to a hospital prison because he needed an operation on his heart. The warden felt that with Harry Daykins gone, there could be serious trouble in the prison because he kept everybody under control – more than the warders could. No more Harry would mean more trouble for the warden and the warders.'

'Oh my giddy aunt!' Sebastian droned again as he began to understand. 'You took 'Arry's place!'

'I didn't want to. I had no choice. The warden said that if I didn't help him out, he would make sure that my life in prison would be horrible! What could I do?'

THE MEN STARED AT MICK INCREDULOUSLY.

'I'm not a gangster. I am a taxi driver. That's all

I've ever been.'

'But you act just like 'Arry Daykins, 'Arry. You act tough like a gangster. You tell everybody what to do and all the inmates are scared of you. *I'm* scared of you!' said Sebastian.

He continued, 'And I *know* Malcolm is frightened to death of you. He thinks you're going to crush him if he doesn't do as you tell him!'

MICK MANAGED A SMILE.

The thought of him sitting on Malcolm, trying to crush him, was hysterical.

'Warden Banks and the warders taught me what to do, and what to say, and how to say it,' Mick explained.

'It took me ages. I had to go to the Warden's office every day to practice. He told me I had to keep acting as Harry until the real Harry came back.'

HE LOOKED AT THEM, TRYING TO READ THEIR THOUGHTS.

'I'm due to be released in two months and Harry Crusher Daykins is coming back. That's it.' He looked at each of them.

THERE WAS SILENCE AS EACH OF

THEM TRIED TO UNDERSTAND WHAT THIS MEANT.

'So, let me get this straight,' Duttan summed up, 'you, Mick, are due to leave prison in two months. A free man.'

'Yes, that's right. Two months,' Mick replied.

'So we've broke you out of prison...'

Mick held up his hand. 'From now on, can we call it the SAS lads? SAS. Please don't mention *'prison'* in front of the children.'

Malcolm continued, 'So we've broke you out of the SAS and you was due to be leavin' anyway in two months?'

'Yes. You are the best friends I have ever had and I know you were only doing your best for me, but accidentally you've completely wrecked everything! I was coming home in June anyway!'

MICK WAS DISTRAUGHT.

A small tear slid down Malcolm's cheek. 'I'm so sorry, 'Arry,' Malcolm said miserably, wiping away the tear, and they all stared at the flames.

'If you remember, I tried to stop you when you told

me about your escape plan.'

DUTTAN NODDED.

'But you insisted it would be easy and we could all stay together on the outside and have a better life away from all the villains in prison.'

DUTTAN NODDED AGAIN.

'You even suggested we could go to live in Zimbabwe, Duttan! Remember?'

DUTTAN FORCED A WEAK SMILE.

'You were so determined to get us all out of prison. I couldn't say anything to stop you because it would have blown my cover. What could I do? I *had* to go along with it.'

For what seemed a long time, nobody spoke. Nobody knew what to say. There was just **SO** much to think about.

'So just *why* were you thrown in prison then, Harry?' Duttan muttered. 'What was your crime?'

'Yeah, wotchyou in for, 'Arry?'

'Bank robbery,' he replied.

'You robbed a bank?' Sebastian asked.

'No. Not exactly. I was hired as a taxi driver by

some blokes to drive them to the bank then to the airport on their holidays. It turned out they were *robbing* the bank and they got caught. The police arrested me as part of the gang.'

'No way! Oh my giddy aunt,' said Sebastian.

'That's not fair!' Malcolm yelled.

Duttan sat **biting** his lip and slowly shook his head, deep in thought.

Mick decided to break the tension, 'I'll go and see if the food is ready, lads.'

He knew this would give them a chance to talk amongst themselves. He had no idea what they would decide to do and he was worried by that fact.

What would they do?

He opened the kitchen door and everyone turned to look at him.

'Becky, I need your help,' he said, indicating with his head that she needed to follow him.

Once she had closed the kitchen door behind her Mick whispered, 'We need to talk, but not here in the hall.' He looked around.

'Follow me,' Becky said and led the way into the snug, a small room next to the kitchen.

Mick closed the door and Becky immediately gave him a **KISS**.

Then she stood back and gave him *'the look'*.

'What is happening, Mick? Are you mad or just trying to wreck our lives?!' **SHE WAS ANGRY**, and then her eyes welled up.

'Shh,' Mick soothed. 'Let me explain.' He tried to hold her, but she pushed him away.

'You'd better, and this had better be good!' she hissed.

He told her how the warden had forced him to pretend to be Harry Daykins, and how he had become so good at the impersonation that all the prison inmates were scared of him. They really thought that he was Harry 'Crusher' Daykins.

He told her how, at first, he was so bad at acting like a villain that he thought he would be found out, but the warden made him practice every day – **FOR HOURS!** The warden needed him to be successful at being Harry Daykins.

'Why did he want you to be Harry Daykins?' Becky interrupted.

'Because prison is full of villains. Most of them are **not** nice and will cause trouble at any time. The warden was worried that the prisoners might become violent and cause him problems. But he knew that they were all scared of Harry Daykins and they wouldn't cause any trouble if they knew he was in their prison.'

Mick explained how he had made friends with three men who had become his 'minders'.

'Duttan is a university graduate from Zimbabwe. He was an accountant who had been caught *'fiddling the books!'* He told me he wanted to be rich!' Mick added with a laugh. 'Don't we all!'

Becky tried to smile, but it looked more like a **grimace**.

'Then, there's Sebastian who enjoys dressing up in ladies clothes and singing. He was caught robbing a ladies clothes store,' Mick continued.

'Finally, there's Malcolm. Loveable Malcolm. He's just a dim-witted bloke who cannot hold onto any job because of his stupidity. As a result, he became a petty criminal – stealing anything he wanted, mostly food and drink – but he was regularly caught and thrown in the '*nick*.'

The three men had become Harry's '**MINDERS**' protecting him from any inmate wanting to cause trouble. They were the three biggest men in the prison.

'They have only ever known me as the gangster Harry Daykins who is due to be in prison for many years. Duttan planned the jailbreak brilliantly. He thought he was saving us all from prison. He thought he was doing me a *huge* favour and that *I, "Harry Daykins"*, would be able to take care of them all on the outside. Of course, they did not know at that time who I really am, just Mick Shufflett, a simple taxi driver.'

Becky listened intently. **ALL OF THIS WAS NEW TO HER.**

'I could not tell them the truth because it would have meant letting them know that I wasn't the *real* Harry Daykins. And, Warden Banks would have been very angry with me!'

'Those men in there are going to be very angry

with you. You know that don't you?' Becky sniffed and wiped her eyes.

'Yes, I know.'

In the lounge, the three men had been **arguing**.

'I can't believe he ain't 'Arry,' Malcolm droned. 'He's been our boss for so long.'

He waved his arms in the air. 'I don't care if he ain't 'Arry, he's still our boss!' he shouted.

'Shh. Keep it down!' Duttan shushed.

'That's right, Malcolm,' Sebastian retorted. 'But it doesn't alter the fact that he *isn't* Harry. What's he going to do now to look after *us*? The *real* Harry would know what to do. He would have some **SECRET** places where we could hide until the heat dies down.'

'He's looked after me better than me own mum!' Malcolm whined.

'Yes, we've all got a lot to thank him for,' Duttan joined in, 'but I think we might have to cut him loose now.'

'Wotchyou mean?' Malcolm looked horrified and angry.

'We might have to leave him here and go our own way,' Duttan explained.

'What? Where to? Where could we go to be safe?' Malcolm snapped. 'I can't go home. Me mum wouldn't be able to feed me!'

'Malcolm is right. We can't go home because that's the first place the police will look,' Duttan observed.

'Well, what are we going to do?' Sebastian grumbled.

'We can't stay here because Harry is clearly *not* Harry. So, we have to make a new plan,' Duttan suggested.

'We didn't have a back-up plan, Dutt, you know that,' Sebastian muttered.

'No, that's true, but it doesn't stop us from planning one now, does it?' he replied.

'Nah,' said Malcolm.

'No,' Sebastian added. 'Have you got something in mind?'

'No, not yet. *That* will depend on your answer to my next question,' Duttan smiled, staring at them.

'And your question is?' Sebastian enquired.

'Yeah. What you finkin', Dutt?' Malcolm said.

'How did you feel about being in prison?'

THERE WAS TOTAL SILENCE AS BOTH MEN MEASURED THE IMPLICATION OF THE QUESTION. They both began to think what prison meant to them and Malcolm replied first.

'It's nice and warm,' said Malcolm, 'with plenty of food.'

'Well, with you two lads and Harry around to look after me, it wasn't such a bad place,' Sebastian replied. 'Right now, if I was being honest, I've got to say that's where I would rather be. Sorry, but it's true!'

I'm glad you both answered positively because I think the only thing we can do now is . . .'

He tormented them, WAITING, WAITING. **HE NIBBLED AT A FINGER NAIL TO ADD TENSION.**

'Is wot?' Malcolm grunted.

He studied them both carefully before adding, 'Is to go back to Moldham.'

Malcolm and Sebastian stared at him, frozen solid like statues, in disbelief.

'We have nowhere else to go,' he went on. 'The police would soon find us anyway. They aren't stupid. Where are we going to go? Where could we hide? We would most probably freeze to death out there in the snow. We have no money. How would we live?'

'We could rob a bank,' Malcolm said.

'Malcolm you couldn't rob a child's piggy box without getting caught!' Sebastian mocked.

'Harry's no use to us now, out here. Out of Moldham,' Duttan continued. 'Inside, he is the Boss. He is in charge and, besides...' he looked at them regretfully.

'What?' Sebastian asked.

'It's our fault that he is in this situation now. We got him into this mess,' Duttan added ruefully.

MALCOLM NODDED AND BEGAN TO BITE HIS NAILS.

'If we're smart and move quickly, we can probably get back inside before the warders spot that we are missing,' Duttan said with only a little bit of conviction.

He stared at them. 'If we don't, we'll either get caught or freeze to death. What do you say?'

Sebastian and Malcolm took their time. They looked at each other then looked back at Duttan.

'OK by me,' Malcolm said.

Sebastian nodded his approval. 'What's your plan?' he asked.

'Well, first of all, we must decide what we are going to do about Harry,' Duttan pointed out.

'Wotchyou mean, "*do about 'Arry?*"' Malcolm said aggressively. 'He's our boss. He looks after us an' *we* look after '*im!*'

'I've got to be honest here, Dutt, I always liked 'Arry but I like him even more now I know he ain't a villain. He's a nice bloke – not like us – and I want him to carry on looking after us when we're back inside! He makes me feel good about myself. He lets me sing.'

'Duttan grinned. 'He gets my vote too, lads. One for all, and all for one!'

'Wassat mean, Dutt?'

'It means 'Arry is still the boss,' Sebastian replied grinning too.

'One for all, and all for one!' said Sebastian and Duttan together.

'Yeah!' Malcolm hissed, **punching** the air. 'Yeah! Let's stick together!'

'So, what are you going to do now, Mick?' Becky asked.

'I don't know,' Mick said dejectedly. 'All I can think of is to give myself up and go back to prison.'

'They will make you stay in prison longer. Maybe an extra two years. You know that!'

'Yes, I know but what else can I do? When the warden realises we're not in our cells, he will come looking for us. So, I must help the lads get away safely and fast.'

He was PENSIVE for a moment then said, 'I'm going to stay here when the lads make a break for it and I'll ring the police tonight when they have got clean away.'

BECKY GAVE HIM A HUG. SHE WAS CRYING NOW.

'I have left the lads to talk it over together while I tell you what has happened. They are going to hate me now. I'd better go and see what they have decided.

Is the food ready?'

BECKY NODDED, UNABLE TO SPEAK.

Mick returned to the lounge. He closed the door behind him and stood leaning against it, scrutinizing the faces of the three men who were staring back at him.

No one spoke.

He tried to read the expressions on their faces and decided to speak first.

'The food is ready, lads,' he announced.

'Cor blimey, great!' Malcolm said, grinning and rubbing his hands together. 'I'm starving.'

Slowly, cautiously, Mick sat back down in his chair by the log fire, waiting for the inevitable backlash from his former **'MINDERS'**. He studied Duttan's face first.

'I think I can get us *all* out of this mess, Harry. Mick, I mean. I say, do you mind if I stick with Harry?' Duttan was about to share his idea.

'What are you thinking, Duttan?' Mick queried with a look of hope and a feeling of some relief.

Duttan often came up with **BRILLIANT** ideas.

'Well, the two van drivers are still tied up in the back of the laundry van with the dirty laundry.'

Mick interrupted him. 'Oh good grief, the two laundry men! They will be half frozen to death! We've got to get them out of there and into the warmth.'

'No, don't panic, Harry. They are tied up in those sheets in a warm van. They will be OK. We didn't hurt them. Malcolm only **THREATENED** to hurt them if they did not co-operate.'

'That's true,' Mick agreed. 'So what's your plan?'

'Well, you are our boss and we all want to keep it that way. We want us to stick together. One for all and all for one! So, this is my plan . . .'

CHAPTER EIGHTEEN
Going Back

'What's it like in the SAS?' Sylvester asked. 'Yes, come on you lot, spill the beans,' Orlando added. 'I've got a commando jacket and me and Sylvester play at being in the SAS all the time.'

Nearly everyone was **jammed** into the lounge, crammed onto the settee and comfy chairs. Dad and Malcolm had brought more chairs from the kitchen and Arthur had built up the fire.

'Are there any women in the SAS?' asked Channing. She was thinking that if it really was exciting then she might join when she got older, or she could write a story about the SAS.

'I'm afraid we can't tell you anything,' Sebastian replied.

'It's classified,' Duttan added.

'Yeah, we'd have to break both your legs,' Malcolm said with delight, **cracking** his knuckles.

'And your arms,' said Sebastian, building the fear further.

'And put 'orrible sticky tape over your mouth to stop you screaming!' Malcolm was loving this.

'We would have to tie you up in a ball too,' Duttan said seriously.

'And throw you in a ditch to be eaten alive by the red ants!'

Sylvester looked **horrified** and Tyrone clung tightly to Dad, burying his face in Dad's chest.

'Now I know you're lying,' said Orlando, 'because we don't have any flesh-eating red ants in this country!'

SYLVESTER LOOKED RELIEVED.

'Who said anything about *this* country?' Sebastian growled. 'We go all over the world.'

'Where there *are* flesh-eating red ants!' Duttan said wide-eyed to add to the tension.

TOTAL SILENCE.

Then all the men burst out laughing and everyone

joined in with some relief.

Orlando loved it. **What a trick.** He might use it himself if he ever got the chance.

Ma had remained in the kitchen with Arthur and Margaret. She was holding Beyonsay.

'You have been so kind and helpful today, Arthur and Margaret, and I know I would not have coped without you. Thank you so much. This is an awful mess.'

Ma put Beyonsay into her high chair with a biscuit and retold the situation to them just as Mick had explained it to her. She told them why he had been in prison, how they had broken out, and how Mick was going to give himself up later when the men had left.

Ma broke down in **FLOODS** of tears and was inconsolable. Margaret held her tightly and Arthur quietly left them and went to join the others in the lounge.

'Did you like our pond?' Orlando asked. 'I tried it myself last week and it's really cold and dirty.'

'That's the first *real* bath we have had in a month,' announced Duttan.

'Yeah, we've been out in the desert for weeks, sweatin' and stinkin',' said Malcolm.

'Speak for yourself, Malcolm,' said Duttan. He lifted his arm up high. 'I never stink.' He took a deep breath under his arm and pulled a face. 'On second thoughts . . .' and began laughing again.

THE CHILDREN WERE BEGINNING TO ENJOY THEMSELVES.

'You remind me of Humpty Dumpty,' Tyrone said pointing to Malcolm and everybody laughed, except Tyrone. He did not realise that he had said something funny.

'Do you know,' Malcolm replied. 'That's the nicest fing anyone has ever said to me!' They all laughed again.

'So, *your* name is Malcolm,' Channing said, trying to get to know more about these huge men.

'Yes, Modam,' said Malcolm, bowing slightly. 'Malcolm Horatio Angel *hat* your service. Me muvver named me after the famous Horatio Nelson what won the Battle of Hastings, 'cos she fought I would be a sailor when I grew up 'cos we used to live near the sea in Watford.'

All the adults hooted with laughter.

'Do you mean Trafalgar?' Channing asked. 'The Battle of Trafalgar?'

'Watford is *nowhere near* the sea!' Orlando joined in. 'Tell him, Arthur. You used to live there, right?'

Malcolm did not seem to hear and carried on. 'Of course, *she* didn't know that I get sea-sick just sitting in the *bath*!' he roared and crossed his eyes, sticking his tongue way out.

'We know who you all are because you introduced everyone to us, Duttan, remember?' Channing said politely. 'At the top of the hill.'

'Yes, I do remember. My name is Duttan Yahmunha and I come from a very small town in Zimbabwe. It's called Murambinda and my parents work at the hospital. It is very pretty,' he said a little dreamily, remembering.

'Sebastian Axel Bowdler. That's me,' said Sebastian. He was still wearing the dressing gown, shower cap and slippers. He spoke into the hairbrush as though it was a microphone. 'Pleased to meet you all.' He looked around and smiled, waving the hair brush. 'My *real* name's Perry, but I changed it myself 'cos I didn't think that Perry was a strong enough name for a burglar. Sebastian sounds much better, don't you agree?'

'Are you a **real** burglar?' asked Sylvester wide-eyed.

'No,' said Dad hurriedly. 'What he means is, for an SAS soldier to *catch* burglars, he has to have a strong name.' Dad glared at Sebastian.

'Sorry, 'Arry,' muttered Sebastian under his breath.

'Why are they calling you Harry, Dad?' Channing could not resist asking the one question on everyone's mind.

Duttan came to Dad's rescue. 'It's a code. All the high-ranking officers have to have a code name in case of capture.'

'Yes, that's it,' Dad approved, and threw Duttan a thankful glance.

Ma and Margaret quietly entered the lounge and

sat down to join in. Ma's eyes were red, but only Dad noticed. Margaret was holding the Bab.

'Do you have to shoot people in the SAS?' Sylvester asked.

'No! Certainly not!' Duttan replied. 'We only shoot people who are *not* in the SAS!'

They all roared with laughter again.

'Have you ever killed anyone?' Sylvester persisted.

'We are not allowed to talk about our missions. We had to sign the Official Secrets Act,' Dad pointed out.

'I've heard of that,' said Orlando. 'All the IMPORTANT people like the prime minister have to sign it.'

'Can't you just say *"yes"* or *"no"*?' Sylvester persevered.

'Do you know what would happen to us if we broke the Official Secrets Act?' Duttan intervened. 'They would send us to prison for the rest of our lives with only dehydrated water to drink and dry bread to eat.'

'Well, you wouldn't be in prison for long then,'

Orlando countered.

'Why is that young man?' Duttan queried.

'Because you would be dead! You can't live on just dry bread. You would die!'

THE MEN LAUGHED AGAIN.

'You're sharp, you are,' said Malcolm. 'Just like your Dad.'

Sebastian held up one hand and put his finger to his lips. He spoke very quietly to create an atmosphere of danger. 'Let me tell you, Orlando, we are highly trained. Isn't that right, lads?'

They nodded.

'We are highly skilled and have been taught to live without proper food for as long as a mission takes. It could be months!'

He looked around for more approval. They all nodded again, solemnly.

'We had to learn how to live off whatever the land provides. So, when we are in the desert there is *no* food at all for us to eat. There is no water to drink. We have to wring out our socks and drink our own sweat.' He looked at the others again. 'Is that right, lads?'

Dad nodded.

'True,' whispered Duttan.

'Nuffink at all,' Malcolm murmured very quietly. 'Only sweat.'

Almost in a whisper, Sebastian carried on. 'So, we have to dig down into the sand with our bare hands until we find cockroaches and worms and dung beetles and desert rats and scorpions.'

He was speaking so quietly now that the children had to lean forwards to hear him.

'Do you know what we do then?' he breathed, almost silently.

Sylvester shook his head.

'WE RUN LIKE MAD!' he yelled at the top of his voice.

Everyone leapt backwards in **shock** and the men **roared** with laughter. Beyonsay began to cry and Ma soothed her tears.

The children recovered and began to laugh too.

'Yeah, and do you know what we do then?' Sebastian continued.

The children leaned back away from him expecting

another outburst.

'We take our packed lunches out of our bags. We can't go hungry, can we?'

ORLANDO CLAPPED. 'That was an amazing trick, Sebastian! You had us all fooled.'

'You certainly cannot go hungry,' said Ma. 'So, Harry, get your lads into the kitchen for some food, then we will see if their clothes are ready to put back on. I can't stand the sight of all this hairy bare flesh any longer!'

The men **grabbed** a chair each and Dad led them to the kitchen, accompanied by Arthur and Margaret.

Ma called for silence and explained to the children that they had to remain in the lounge and watch TV or play games, without killing each other, while she got the men organised in the kitchen.

'I wonder what it's like to shoot a real gun,' Sylvester speculated, aiming an **_imaginary_** gun at the TV when she had gone.

Orlando turned it on and began searching the channels.

*

Across the hall in the kitchen, Ma handed the Bab to Margaret, while she went to check the men's clothing.

'D'you fink this is gonna work, Dutt?'

'Of course it will work,' Duttan replied very confidently. 'Now, let's eat, get dressed and put the plan into action as soon as we can. We are running short of time.'

Margaret and Arthur SERVED the food and the men ate **hungrily**. They had seconds, thirds and fourths!

'Blimey, these lads know how to eat, Mick!' Arthur joked. 'I'm glad I don't have to feed them every day!'

Mick grinned back at him and that was the moment Arthur remembered where he had seen Mick previously. But, before he had chance to say anything, Ma came in carrying some folded clothes. 'Well, you'll be glad to know that they are all clean and dry,' she told them. She held them to her face. 'And they are still warm.'

She handed them to Mick and went back for the rest.

Mick checked the **NAME TAGS** on each item and gave the clothes to the men. When everyone had their clothes, they went upstairs to put them on.

Five minutes later, they were all back in the kitchen and Duttan ran through his plan.

'So, Malcolm goes up to get the van. I will go with him to check on the two drivers.'

'What drivers?' Ma asked.

'I will explain later, Mrs... Becky,' he answered.

'I don't fink I can get it down in this snow,' said Malcolm.

'Malcolm, you are the best driver we have. If anyone can get that van down here, it's you. Anyway, I will be with you so, if you crash, you will not be on your own!' Duttan was trying all his powers of persuasion.

Malcolm was **NOT** convinced.

'We don't have any other choice,' Sebastian added. 'Malcolm, it's up to you.'

'Just a minute. 'Arry, didn't you say you been a taxi driver all your life?' Malcolm was having a bright idea and Mick began to wonder if it was going to be a bad one.

'Well, yes I have,' Mick replied slowly.

'Well, that's it,' Malcolm cracked his knuckles. 'You are a hexpert. You should drive the van.'

Duttan **snapped** his fingers. 'He has a very good point, boss. You must have driven in all conditions, in all weathers and terrain. Harry, you really are an expert and, Malcolm, you have had a brainwave.'

Malcolm beamed.

'Yeah, so remember that. It's your first ever!' Sebastian laughed. 'I'm gonna put a note in my diary, when I buy one, to remember this day.'

'But I've never driven a large van before,' said Mick, slightly apprehensive.

'Well, it's got a wheel at each corner and a steering wheel just like a car, hasn't it?' Sebastian pressed home the advantage.

'Well, yes... but...'

'But nuffink, boss. You're the man! You should drive.'

'Harry?' Duttan looked at him, searching for his agreement.

'Harry, Malcolm is right. *You* are the man.' Duttan was determined now.

Mick thought for a moment. 'Do you know, lads, the last time I drove a bunch of big geezers, I ended up in prison.'

They stared at him quizzically.

'And now, I will be doing the exact same thing. I will be driving a bunch of big geezers and ending up in prison. Now that's ironic!'

'What's a *'ronic'*?' Malcolm asked.

Duttan was being rational. 'But, Harry, you have only got two months before you are released anyway. We have got to get you back in before you are missed. Then, you will come out as a free man in June.'

'I know. I understand. Malcolm is right. It's got to be me who drives the van. But – but, that's not my worry though.'

'Come on, Harry. You're the boss,' said Sebastian, joining in. 'The boss shouldn't have to worry. That's what you have us for. We do the worrying for you.'

'Don't you see,' Mick said, looking quite upset, 'by getting me back in, you will be stuck back in prison again. And you've only just broken out. It will be my fault.'

'Oh, don't worry about me,' said Malcolm. 'I like it in prison. I get lots of lovely grub and it's the only place I've ever stayed where the bed is big enough for me! Normally my feet are 'angin' over the end and they don't half get cold.'

'Yeah, I've only got another two years to do anyway,' said Sebastian with a grin.

'I can work another plan and break us out all over again, once you have been released,' Duttan said, laughing. 'We can come and live with you!'

They all **laughed** and Mick felt a little better.

'Besides, Harry, we are doing this as much for ourselves as for you. We don't really have a choice now. If we don't get back inside, we will eventually get caught or freeze to death in this snow!'

'A grim thought,' said Sebastian. 'Let's go back.'

'Okay, let's do this,' he called, rubbing his hands together. 'Are you ready, Duttan?'

'I'm ready, boss. Let's go get the van.'

Using all his experience and driving skills, Mick eased the van down the long, steep lane and into the drive of

Budleigh Cottage where he heaved a sigh of relief.

The men climbed carefully out of the cab and went around to the back of the van. Duttan slowly opened the doors, just in case the two van drivers had got themselves free from the straps around their feet and wrists. They were still safely tied and lying under a pile of laundry.

Malcolm and Sebastian came out and they each **slung** one of the drivers over their shoulder and carried them into the kitchen. They **dropped** them on a chair and the men looked up at them, frightened.

Margaret looked on, **horrified,** before she recovered her composure. Arthur had his arm around her shoulder.

'Are you lads hungry?' she asked, handing cutlery and dishes to Arthur to place in front of the two men.

They nodded.

'Good. We've got some lovely soup and toast for you here,' she said with a CALMING smile.

Duttan spoke to them both. 'Now, before you get any food, you have got to *listen* to what I have to tell you, and you must *agree* to what I ask you. Is that OK?'

'Or I'll have to book you into a hospital bed!' Malcolm **CRACKED** his knuckles.

'Malcolm, that's enough! These men are our friends. Aren't you lads?' Mick smiled at them.

'Sorry, 'Arry.'

The two men nodded.

'You can talk to us, lads,' Duttan continued. 'Do you understand?'

'Yes, we understand,' they chorused.

'Okay, now I am going to remove your bindings, so that you are more comfortable and can eat your food. If you try to run for it, I will be forced to get my two friends here to sit on you. You will not like that.'

One of the men nodded, the other shook his head.

'Harry, it's time for you to go and tell the children that we are going back out on the mission, but you will see them in two months' time when you finish with the SAS for good.'

'I'm on it, Duttan. I will leave you to explain to our two new friends here what we expect of them.' He glanced at the two men and gave them a cool 'thumbs up'.

In the lounge a wrestling match was underway. Orlando and Sylvester were **locked** together with Tyrone sitting on top, ***bouncing*** up and down. Channing was writing in a large note pad.

'Okay everybody, let's be friends for five minutes and sit still. I need to tell you something,' Dad called out.

When the children were sitting still Dad began. 'Now, as you know, I am on a secret mission at the moment with the team, and it is time for us to get moving and complete it.'

'Where are you going next, Dad?' asked Orlando.

'I'm not able to answer that, sorry. Just listen and

I will try to explain.'

In the kitchen, Duttan was putting the final touches to the return plan.

'So, are you clear now on what you have to do, lads?'

'Yes, Duttan,' said John the van driver.

'Yes, Duttan,' said Pete the other van driver.

'Good,' said Duttan giving one of his biggest smiles. 'And are you clear on what will happen to you both if you don't get it right?'

'Yes, Duttan,' said Pete.

'Yes, Duttan,' said John.

'Good.' Duttan flashed another huge smile. 'This is going to be easy. We like these two lads, don't we, boys?'

'They are our friends now,' Malcolm said.

'I've liked them ever since I tied them up this morning,' Sebastian purred.

Harry returned.

'Is everything on schedule here? No hiccups?'

'No hiccups, Harry. Everything is on schedule,'

Duttan responded.

'Good, we need to get going now if we are to collect the clean laundry and get back to Moldham in time.'

Mick looked at Arthur and Margaret. 'I can't thank you two enough for all your help with my family. I'm sorry if we have put you under a strain today. We didn't mean to. I'm looking forward to meeting you when I get back in June.'

Arthur and Margaret **smiled** back at him and Margaret gave him a **HUG.** Arthur reached out and the two men shook hands.

Mick turned to Becky. She was crying silently and handed Beyonsay to Margaret. 'Please be careful,' she said. 'We don't want any mistakes now.'

'I will do my best,' he answered and gave her a hug. They kissed.

'We must go, Harry,' Duttan hassled.

Malcolm and Sebastian helped John and Pete to their feet and led them out of the kitchen into the hall.

Arthur held up his hand to stop them. 'Just a minute, lads. Do you think I could have a quick word with John and Pete?' he asked.

The two convicts looked at him a little warily.

'Please,' Arthur was insistent. 'On their own.'

Harry looked at Duttan then nodded in approval and Arthur closed the kitchen door to talk to John and Pete alone.

'We are going!' shouted Dad. The children **charged** out of the lounge. 'Okay. Have you got everything clear in your minds?'

'Yes, Dad,' said Sylvester.

'Of course, sir,' said Orlando, saluting.

'Of course, sir,' said Tyrone, copying.

'Sure have, Dad.' Channing was trying to smile.

'I'm going to miss you lot.' Dad choked. 'Okay, now, remember, *this* is "Operation Soap Bubbles" and *you* are Command HQ. *We* are Mission Patrol. Your Ma will get a text when the mission is completed. It will be in SAS jargon and it will say...?'

'Bubbles burst!'

they all shouted together.

'Good. Now what does it mean if the message

states, '*Bubbles floating*?'

'Operation failed,' they called.

'But it won't,' Orlando added.

'You've got it!' Dad said. 'Now let's have a smart salute from everybody and I have got to go.'

They all saluted and Dad turned to leave.

'Dad!' Channing called.

He turned and she leapt at him, **THROWING** her arms around his neck, squeezing him tight.

She whispered, 'Dad, please be careful. I love you!' Unseen, she placed a folded piece of paper in his pocket and ran upstairs.

Dad watched her go then held out his arms and had a group hug with the boys.

'Harry!' Duttan called.

John and Pete came out of the kitchen and Dad led his three 'minders' outside where they scrambled into the back of the van. John and Pete closed the doors and climbed into the cab.

The van moved off slowly through the **THICK** snow on the drive.

*

'What was that with John and Pete?' Margaret asked as the van disappeared.

'Just a little bit of insurance,' Arthur grinned. 'Just making sure the drivers know which side to be on.'

'What have you been doing, Arthur?'

'When I heard the two drivers talking, it was obvious that they were Brummies. The only thing I wasn't sure of was whether they were Blues fans or Villa fans. When they told me they were *"blue noses"* I was so relieved and decided to do a little *"bribing"* to make sure they were on our side.'

'You're taking them to a match, aren't you?'

'Quite right, m'dear. Next Saturday against Bristol City and they will be sitting with me in the directors' box. My treat. Might even see if Trevor Francis can meet us there. That's where I had seen Mick before. He used to go to every home match until he joined the SAS!'

CHAPTER NINETEEN
Band on the Run

'**A**nything yet, Ma?' Orlando enquired. 'They've only been gone ten minutes, Orlando! Give them a chance.'

This was going to be a long and difficult wait. 'It's so boring just waiting!' moaned Orlando.

'There's nothing to do.' He could not even force himself to find Sylvie for a fight.

'Why don't you take the Bab into the lounge and build a tower or do a jigsaw with her?'

Under normal circumstances, he would rather have pulled out his toe nails and eaten them with **GREEN CABBAGE** than build a tower with the Bab. But these were not normal circumstances. He had to find a way to pass the time until the text message came through.

'Nah... oh, why not? Bee, do you want to come and build a castle with Orly?'

'Orly, cass,' she mimicked.

'Beyonsay!' Ma corrected him. 'Her name is Beyonsay.'

'OK, Ma. Don't wet your knickers!'

'You'll get a clip in a minute.' She was smiling – a kind of worried smile – and he knew she was thinking hard and worrying about Dad. Ma was grateful to get *any* help with looking after the baby.

'Come on,' Orlando said, lifting Beyonsay out of her high chair. 'Hold on tight.'

She put her arms around his neck and wrapped her legs around his waist.

'Clever girl.' He smiled at her then she put her hands over his eyes. 'Bee, I can't see!' he cried.

'Beyonsay!' Ma roared.

'No see! No see!' Beyonsay giggled.

Orlando could not let go in order to move her hands because she would have **fallen** backwards to the floor. So, he kept his eyes tightly shut and began to work his way towards the kitchen door slowly and very carefully.

After only three cautious steps, Beyonsay lifted her hands from his eyes and called 'Pee po!' Her nose was close up against his own.

'Pee po,' he answered, waiting for her hands to cover his eyes again.

Instead, she grabbed his ears. And yanked **HARD!**

'Aaargh!' he screamed, looking for a place to put her down safely. The door to the lounge was still open, so he ran to the settee where he was able to lower her gently onto her back so that he could prise her fingers from his ears.

'You might be a little one, but you're very strong, aren't you?'

'Stong,' said Beyonsay, trying to copy him.

He covered her eyes and played "Pee po" with her several times. 'Now, what shall we do?' he asked. 'Shall we build a tower or do a jigsaw puzzle?'

He had just rebuilt the tower for the sixth time, when he heard Ma's mobile phone '*ping*'.

Orlando listened intently, waiting for Ma to relay the message. Beyonsay **smashed** the tower in one sweep of her arm. Ma came out of the kitchen towards him looking desolate.

'What is it?' he asked, but he knew what was coming next from the look on her face.

'*Bubbles floating!*' Ma whispered weakly.

Orlando stared at his mother across the hall and called the others to come down. '*Bubbles floating!*' he called.

Channing led the way and stopped at the bottom of the stairs searching their faces. The phone rang.

'Hello,' said Ma nervously. She waited. 'Oh no!'

She listened for a long time in silence then said, 'Leave it with me. I will do what I can. Give me a few minutes and... stay warm.' She clicked off her phone and looked at the children who were now worried and frightened.

'They are stuck in a deep snowdrift, on the bend in the lane just past the bus stop. The snow is as deep as the wheels of the van. The wheels keep skidding and they have tried to dig it out with their hands, but it is too deep and their hands are freezing.'

'Have we got any shovels in the shed, Ma?' Orlando

asked. 'We can take them to Dad.'

'You are not going anywhere now. It's getting dark and it will be below freezing out there.'

While she spoke, Ma was checking her 'contacts' list and finally found the one she wanted. She waited for an answer.

'Hello, Margaret. It's Becky. We have heard from Mick and it is not good news, I'm afraid.'

She listened. 'No, nothing like that. They are stuck in a snowdrift near the end of the lane.'

She waited again. 'Yes, *our* lane! They have only gone about a mile. They can't get out of the snow. Do you think you could you ask Cecil to go and help them with his tractor, please?'

Fifteen minutes later, **bright**, **flashing** yellow lights signalled the arrival of Cecil's huge tractor as it pulled up outside Budleigh Cottage. Everyone raced to the door to tell Cecil where to look for the van.

'They're on their way!' Cecil said, grinning.

'Do you mean that you've got them out already?' Orlando asked incredulously.

'I sure have,' he replied. 'Piece of cake. Was nothing. Only took two minutes.'

'Wow! I want one of those tractors when I grow up,' Tyrone said, giving teddy a view of the huge machine through the window. It had two very bright headlights and three flashing yellow lights.

Ma made Cecil a **HOT** cup of tea as he explained what had happened. 'Once I attached my tow bar, I pulled them up to the main road about six hundred metres away. The main road was pretty much clear of snow, so they shouldn't have any more problems.' He slurped loudly on his cup of tea. Sylvester and Orlando found it very funny and grinned.

'What I thought strange was '*What's a Moldham Prison van doing out here?*'' he added.

'Moldham *SAS* van,' said Ma. 'SAS van, Cecil.' She put a finger to her lips and pointed at the children.

Cecil caught on quickly and copied Ma, 'Oh I see. SAS, is it?'

'Yes. SAS, Cecil. I think they got lost in the snow and called in here to ask the way,' Ma continued.

Cecil slurped the remainder of his tea and everyone **giggled**. 'Well, I've got to be going now. Thanks for the tea. Much appreciated.'

'Thanks for your help, Cecil. It was very kind of you.' Ma took Cecil's arm and led him to the door.

'No Problem. Glad to be of help. I hope those lads get back to the...' He looked at Ma.

'SAS, Cecil,' she prompted him.

'Yeah, I hope they get back to the SAS, OK.'

'How long should it take them from now, Cecil?'

'Oh only about an hour and a half if they don't get stuck again. Should be back by half past seven, I reckon.'

They watched the tractor disappear down the drive towards the lane.

'So, we should get our message from Dad at about half past seven,' Ma told the children.

'In the meantime, Orlando, you and Tyrone can play with Beyonsay, and Channing and Sylvester can help me in the kitchen.'

Channing had other ideas. 'It's OK, Ma. Let Sylvester play with the others. You and I can manage in the kitchen on our own.'

Ma did not like dissent, but it had been a very difficult day and she was TIRED and, more importantly, **worried**.

She submitted. 'All right,' she agreed.

Sylvester did not need to be asked twice. He leapt into the lounge with the others. As soon as Sylvester closed the door to the lounge behind him, Channing closed the kitchen door to be alone with her mother.

She did not waste any time. 'He's in prison, Ma, isn't he?'

Ma **GAZED** at her.

'Please tell me the truth.'

Ma continued to stare back at Channing.

'I've thought for a long time that he was *not* in the SAS.'

Ma looked at her, not knowing what to say.

'He *is* in prison, Ma, isn't he?'

Ma's eyes **welled** up and a tear overflowed. She took a tissue from her sleeve and gently dabbed it away.

'What made you think that?' she managed to ask.

'Well, for a start, we never have enough money. If Dad was in the SAS he would receive wages, wouldn't he?'

Ma looked but said nothing.

'And – you always *read* Dad's letters to us and never let us *see* them. But, you left one out on the table once and I read it. It was on Moldham *Prison* notepaper.'

Ma looked **HORRIFIED.** 'And you didn't say anything?'

'No, I was too scared. I put it on your bedside cabinet to make you think no one could have seen it.'

'All soldiers get to go home on holiday, don't they? So, why not Dad? That letter explained why he never comes home to visit his own family.'

Ma nodded, beginning to realise her daughter's understanding of the situation.

Channing continued. 'He wasn't here for Beyonsay when she was born. Surely the army would let him come home for something as important as a new baby.'

'Then, today, there have been far too many mentions of prison for it to be an accident, and I watched you trying to cover it up each time.'

'OK, stop,' Ma said holding up her hand.

Channing ignored her and continued, 'Ma, you

have been amazing today and it must have been so difficult for you. I don't know how you have coped all this time. I have always *thought* that you are amazing, but now I *know* it!'

Ma put her arms around Channing and gave her a hug. They both dabbed away tears.

'Don't tell your brothers, will you?' Ma whispered. 'Orlando would be devastated if he knew.'

'I think he knows already, Ma.'

'What do you mean? How?' Ma asked, looking very concerned.

'Well, he is *so* proud of Dad being in the SAS but, he has said to me a few times that it is strange that Dad never comes home on leave. Or why we haven't ever got any money. And now, today, he said to me '*Why are they wearing blue boiler suits instead of combats?*'

'Oh dear, what a mess!' said Ma with a sigh.

They sat down at the table.

'*Why* is he in prison, Ma?'

'It was an accident. He picked up some men in his taxi and took them to a bank. He didn't know it but they were *robbing* the bank! They told him to wait for them and to drive them to the airport afterwards.'

'He had bank robbers in his taxi?'

Ma nodded. 'They came out of the bank with the bags of money and jumped into Dad's taxi and, just as he started to drive away, the police surrounded the car.'

'So they thought he was part of the gang?' Channing summed it up beautifully.

'Yes, that's *exactly* what they thought,' Ma replied.

'Oh, Ma, what a mess! So, for almost two years, Dad has been innocent and stuck in prison!'

'I'm afraid so,' said Ma, 'and there's nothing we

can do about it.'

'Well, when he comes home, we are going to find a way to prove he is innocent. When does he come home, Ma?'

'Officially, he is released in two months' time. So, right now, they are trying to sneak back into prison before anyone knows they have broken out. That's what "*Operation Soap Bubbles*" is all about.'

'They are trying to get back into the prison right now?' Channing enquired.

'Yes, and if they don't get back in unnoticed, they will have to stay in prison for a lot longer for *escaping*.'

'Oh, Ma! This is awful!'

'It certainly is. It could mean another two years in prison if they are caught!'

Fifty-five kilometres away, a white van drove through the darkness along icy roads. John was driving and his co-driver, Pete was checking the navigation. They had collected clean laundry and were now heading back to Moldham Prison.

'We should be there in about half an hour,' said

Pete.

'Let's hope these roads remain clear of snow and ice,' John replied. He looked at the temperature gauge. It showed -4°C outside. 'I hope the gritters have been out tonight,' he added.

Behind them, in the back of the van, the four men in blue boiler suits passed the time away playing *"rock, paper, scissors"* and singing songs. One of their favourite songs was 'Chain Gang' which they sang regularly in Moldham.

There was fresh, clean laundry all around them and it smelled good.

'I'm sorry, lads!' Malcolm cried. 'I'm *so* sorry!'

'What for?' Mick asked. 'What's wrong?'

'It's gonna be bad!' Malcolm wailed.

Sebastian was nearest and got the first whiff. *'Malcolm!'* he yelled. *'Aaarrgh!* You stink!'

Malcolm **RIPPLED** again, noisily, and Mick laughed.

'Look, I said I'm sorry, didn't I?' Malcolm looked at them all as they held their breath and covered their noses with their hands.

'It's those beans we had earlier,' he moaned.

'I'm gagging!' Sebastian screeched when he ran out of breath and had to breathe in. Mick and Duttan were **laughing** as they held their breath.

Malcolm tried to change their attention, 'I spy with my little—' but that was as far as he got because everyone threw bags of laundry at him.

'Malcolm, put a sock in it!' called Sebastian and that is exactly what happened. With **AMAZING** accuracy, Mick managed to throw a sock straight into his mouth.

'It can't be one of your own socks,' said Duttan, 'or you would be unconscious now! Come to think of it, we are nearly unconscious ourselves!'

Sebastian had an idea. 'Hey, lads, what's the name of this song?'

He stood up with his feet spread wide apart just like Elvis Presley and, using a towel, he began to play his 'air' guitar' with great enthusiasm. He opened his mouth and began to sing, 'Warden Banks threw a party in Moldham jail. The prison band was there and they began to wail.'

He stopped and **wiggled** his knees just as John hit the brakes.

Sebastian was catapulted forward to land in a heap on top of Malcolm, causing him to fart loudly again.

'Cor blimey, Seb. Watch what you're doin'. You could've killed me!' Malcolm yelled from underneath the tangled bodies.

'Malcolm, you stink!' Sebastian wailed.

'I know this song,' said Mick, 'because Elvis is one of my favourite singers. It's 'Jailhouse Rock' yes?'

'You got it!' replied Sebastian. 'I love that song!'

'We're here!' Mick whispered.

'OK, let's quickly go over the plan once more. This time it is for *real*,' Duttan murmured. Pete **JUMPED** out and John backed the van up to the loading bay. Pete **waved** at him to stop as it reached the concrete landing. 'Pete will give three bangs on the back door to let us know we must get completely out of sight under the laundry,' Duttan continued.

Bang! Bang! Bang!

They all dived under piles of laundry.

Mick checked everyone and spotted Malcolm's huge bottom sticking up out of the pile. He leaned over and DRAGGED a pair of pyjama bottoms over Malcolm's big bum.

'They will bring four trolley bins to the back doors and we each get into a trolley. They will cover us and wheel us into the laundry,' Duttan completed his instructions.

SOMEONE UNLOCKED THE BACK DOORS OF THE VAN.

'Remember,' said Mick quickly and quietly, 'once inside the laundry, Pete will cough when it's OK to get out of your trolley. *Don't* move until you hear him cough. Then pretend you've been in the laundry all day.'

'OK, 'Arry.'

'Shhhhh!'

Both doors **swung** open wide and there stood Warden Banks with his arms folded. He did not look happy.

JOHN AND PETE STOOD ON EITHER

SIDE OF HIM.

'Bring that pile of towels here to me, John,' he barked.

John walked into the back of the van, SNIFFED and tried not to gag. Behind him, Malcolm trumped. To cover the noise, John said loudly, 'Erm, which pile, Warden?'

He picked up a pile of folded towels. Duttan was nearest and felt the towels brush against him. 'This pile, warden?'

'No, *that* pile there!' Warden Banks bellowed. 'What's the matter with you, John? Anyone would think you've got something hidden in there!'

John put the towels back down and went to pick up another pile.

'Leave it! Come out, John. I'll get them myself.' The warden walked into the van almost tripping over Duttan's legs under a huge pile of uniforms. He looked around, surveying the entire contents of the van.

Under the piles of laundry, everyone held their breath. Mick was **PRAYING** that no one would cough or sneeze, or worse!

'It smells foul in here!' Warden Banks growled. He sniffed hard. 'It's appalling. I thought this clean laundry was supposed to smell really fresh.'

'It does, Warden. Pick up a towel and give it a good sniff,' Pete joined in.

'Oh, yes, it *does* smell fresh,' the Warden agreed, sniffing a clean white bath towel.

He put it down and walked out. 'OK, get this lot out and into the laundry room fast, and get something to spray that van with. It smells like a dead rat has been in there for a month!'

'Yes, Warden Banks,' the two men replied, relieved.

It was eight o'clock when Mick sat on his bed in his prison cell.

He reached into his top pocket for the mobile phone given to him by Duttan. As he took it out, a piece of paper fell on to the bed. He picked it up and held it in his fingers as he typed the all-important message into the phone:

BUBBLES BURST!

He clicked 'send' and the most incredible cheer

went up many kilometres away in Budleigh Cottage.

The boys were **cheering** and *dancing* in a huddle, Beyonsay was BANGING her rattle, Channing was hugging Ma, and Ma was laughing and crying at the same time.

In his cell, Mick opened the piece of paper. It read:

To Dad.

It was amazing to see you today! What a surprise! We all loved having you with us and sliding down the hill. I wish we had known you were coming to see us because we could have made a cake especially for you.

It was such fun with you and your friends. They are so funny and I am glad that they look after you and take care of you.

Please tell them we miss them and we can't wait to see them all again. Dad, I know you are in prison and not the SAS, and I want you to know that I don't care! I just want you to come back home so we can be a family again.

You are a special Dad and we all miss you badly. Please come home soon.

I love you Dad and I miss you., Channing xxxxxx

Alan Stott went to school in Birmingham where he was the smallest kid in his year group but still managed to play in goal for the school football team for five years! He wanted to play in midfield but at the trials he never had the chance. So, he put his hand up for goalie – the only position left!

He studied at Bishop Lonsdale College, Derby, and Nottingham University to become a teacher with a B Ed degree.

He taught in Derby then Solihull, followed by a post in an inner city Birmingham school. He then went into industry for a few years to see what the rest of the world did for a living.

Because he badly missed teaching he returned as a supply teacher. Since then he has taught in Sutton Coldfield as Head of Maths and PE in a middle school where he helped to introduce 'Football in the Community' with Ron Wylie of Aston Villa FC.